WEST OF YESTERDAY

Center Point
Large Print

WEST OF YESTERDAY

William Colt MacDonald

CENTER POINT LARGE PRINT
THORNDIKE, MAINE

For
HENRIETTA M. BROWN

◆ ◆ ◆

This Center Point Large Print edition
is published in the year 2025 by arrangement with
Golden West Inc.

The text of this Large Print edition is unabridged.
In other aspects, this book may vary
from the original edition.
Printed in the United States of America
on permanent paper sourced using
environmentally responsible foresting methods.
Set in 16-point Times New Roman type.

ISBN: 979-8-89164-577-6

The Library of Congress has cataloged this record
under Library of Congress Control Number: 2025932756

CHAPTER 1

Since midmorning the cannonading had been continual, rocking blasts shaking the earth and lighting it with flashes of evil, crimson-yellow light. The guns of the blue-clad Federal forces pounded relentlessly through the murky drizzle in which the two armies had clashed. Repeatedly, the ragged gray lines slogged doggedly forward through the obscuring haze, only to falter again before the devastating fire of Union infantry muskets. Shortly past noon jubilant word was carried to General Sherman's headquarters, near Bentonville, North Carolina, that the Confederates would be finished before nightfall. Actually, the end was nearer, at that moment, than the Union leaders realized.

The Federals were winning the last major conflict of the Civil War, as weakened Confederates fighting beneath tattered banners failed to dent the impenetrable blue lines. The men in gray were pressed back and back until, a panic overtaking them, they broke and fled. Despite bitter cursing by General Johnston's officers, the troops scattered wildly over the rain-drenched land, a majority falling, never to rise again.

Maneuvers of Confederate cavalry proved futile when the break came. Both horses and riders became infected by the contagion of defeat: what had begun as an orderly retreat, was transformed into a chaotic rout, and Southern cavalrymen scattered in wild disorder like tattered bits of old paper whipped crazily in the force of a hurricane.

Even before the final sacrificial charge started, Major Garth Haldane, 8th Texas Cavalry, twice wounded—a chunk of lead in his left shoulder and an angry gash across one thigh—had been ordered to the rear in charge of his sergeant, Judd Taggert. Taggert lashed the major into his saddle; disregarding Haldane's semi-delirious protests, Taggert mounted and, leading the major's animal, started off through the sulfuric fog of rain and powdersmoke. Whining cannon balls and cannister shrieked through the lowering atmosphere, as Taggert sought some place of safety. Capture was to be avoided at all costs right now; Haldane's wounds could receive attention later.

Taggert cursed bitterly and glanced back at Haldane, weaving drunkenly on the horse's back, right hand clutched in the animal's mane. He looked beyond his major and saw with relief that they hadn't been followed. Rain and smoke drifted like tangled veils across the battlefield. The Union forces had scattered the worn-out Confederates as spindrift is flung wildly from a turbulent sea.

"But, by Gawd," he muttered angrily, "there'll

come another day. The blue-belly don't live that can whup a Texan."

He urged the horses across the crest of a low hill and down a long slope between slim pine trunks, running with water. Rain soaked into the two shabby, gray uniforms. The horses panted across wet earth, spongy with pine needles. Haldane's eyes were wide, unseeing. Behind them the sounds of battle were fainter. The light was nearly gone by the time the two riders found shelter in a clump of turkey oak and cedar, leaves beaded heavily with moisture. That night they made a wet camp in a creek bottom choked with willow and briers. Taggert did what was possible for Haldane's wounds. Some parched corn from the major's saddlebags provided the only food.

During the night a Federal patrol passed so closely that the slightest noise from the Confederates would have betrayed them. Dawn was a faint lifting of the night rather than arrived daylight. It was raining harder now. There were no sounds from distant guns. The sky was an expanse of dank, blank gray canvas. Taggert scrambled up from the creek bottom to survey the dim, misty terrain. Outlines were blurred, but far-off he spied faintly the movement of men and horses.

"Headin' for Raleigh like's not," he muttered harshly. "All right. So we're cut off from our regiment. Right now we'll be heading in another direction." He shoved the faded, slouch-brim hat to one side and thoughtfully scratched his head, a swarthy man with dark eyes and hair, unshaven. He returned and started to get the horses ready. Haldane appeared rational enough; some of the pain had lessened. They pushed their mounts up from the creek bottom and went on.

Through the long day they traveled through trees and brush. Haldane was bronzed, with a shock of tawny hair and beard. Their uniforms were patched, faded; their slouch hats dripped moisture. The major wore a long, military cloak, the sergeant, a heavy overcoat that had once belonged to a Union infantryman, though its color had faded to an indiscriminate gray. The horses moved with reluctance. Both men carried cap-and-ball six-shooters in holsters; in addition, Haldane had a cavalry saber dangling at his side. At one time, Taggert had owned a carbine, but arms don't last forever in four years of fighting a war. Many of Terry's Texas Rangers, known as personnel of the 8th Texas Cavalry, had possessed of late only ancient flintlocks and smooth-bore muskets sent from home.

They passed a clump of sweet-gum trees, rivulets of water coursing down the deeply furrowed massive trunks. Taggert drew rein to attend his major. Haldane was now slumped to one side, feverish, eyes wild and bloodshot. Taggert tugged him upright in the saddle. "You'd best grip on a mite tighter, Major. We'll make to find a resting place right soon. Just you hang and rattle a mite. This can't go on much longer."

Haldane made no reply. Taggert doubted he heard the words. He stiffened, sat bolt upright, voice momentarily strong as he called a command. "Forward, Rangers! Front into line! Charge those damned Yanks! Make 'em eat Texas lead . . ." The words dwindled to silence and he slumped again, eyes unseeing. Taggert's dark features were anxious. He'd have to get the major to a bed right soon. But where? It had ceased raining now, but the clouds hung low and heavy. They pushed hopelessly on, now well out of the battle zone.

The long day passed, if it could be called day, this dim, soggy, gray half-light through which they passed. It must have been nearing five in the afternoon when they sloshed up from a stand of long-leaf pine into a small clearing crossed by a narrow, wheel-rutted, puddled road, bordered with patches of wiregrass. Taggert halted the horses, then walked his mount to the center of the road, glancing cautiously in both directions. It was then he saw the building of weathered boards, some hundred feet distant across the road, with tall conifers spreading branches above the moss-spotted shingles. Taggert halted the horse, sitting his saddle very still and alert while he considered the place.

9

It was of wide, two-story construction, with heavy timbers at supporting points. The roof extended from the level of the second floor to cover a wide gallery fronting the entrance. From the gallery roof a rusted iron bracket supported a swinging wood sign, now bullet-riddled and paint-faded. Taggert judged it had been some sort of hostelry. A few shutters still held their place; others were missing, or hung aslant from a single rusted hinge. At the rear, the trees and brush obscured the view. Here, Taggert considered, was shelter of a sort. He studied the two brick chimneys rising from the roof. No smoke there. Yes, the place looked deserted.

Still, Taggert hesitated. Occupying troops of both North and South had swept through this country like locusts. That was war. Taggert frowned, thinking, *I been in view now for at least five minutes. No one has slung lead or even hailed me. If there was civilians there, they'd had a fire on such a day. Hell's bells it must be empty. I reckon it's safe for us to shelter there.* He turned his horse back to the waiting Haldane, slumped in saddle. "Come on, Major, I got us a place to unroll our dunnage a spell. With luck, I might even find a mite of chow and some firewood."

Nearing the building, Taggert slowed the horses, alert for any hostile action. After a moment he breathed easier. Now he would read the words on that battered sign suspended from

the edge of the gallery roof: *The Boar & Tankard.*
Below, in peeling paint, was a representation of a
pewter tankard superimposed with a fierce boar's
head.

Haldane roused and spoke plaintively, "What is
this place, Judd?"

"Old inn of some sort, Major. Looks deserted.
We'll see."

They halted before the gallery fronting the
building, Taggert's sharp eyes slipping over
and around the building. Just the wide double-
doored entrance, now closed; three many-paned
windows on either side, with some glass cracked
or missing altogether. Weeds grew unchecked at
the edge of the gallery floor. A ragged dogwood
tree at one end of the porch, a broken branch
hanging disconsolately, was starting to push
out sparse buds. Taggert dismounted and came
around to help Haldane step down. Impatiently,
Haldane shook him off. Taggert paid no attention
as he unlashed the rope. "You just take it easy,
Major, and mind that shoulder now."

The drenched military cloak had flapped to
one side a moment, and Taggert had a brief
glimpse of the darkened stain on Haldane's left
shoulder above the improvised sling supporting
the helpless left arm. Haldane swayed as his
boots touched the earth, then with an effort of
will stood erect, though Taggert didn't remove
his aiding arm. The reins of both horses had been

dropped to earth, and the two men started toward the gallery steps, Taggert warning, "Watch your step, Major. There's a board missing from them risers."

They crossed the gallery floor, worn down to bare wood. Taggert tried the door handle. It was unlocked. Cautiously he pushed it open a little, the hinges squeaking loudly in the silence, and glanced within.

Haldane sagged against him, eyes only half open, muttering querulously, "What are you waiting for, Judd? We'll pay what is asked . . ."

"Hush, Major. We ain't had any money for a long spell. Anyway, it don't look like anybody is here. I reckon it's all right."

His dark eyes took in such part of the big room as could be seen beyond the opened door, seeing the short counter—perhaps it served as a bar— against the back wall at the opposite, right end, of the room. At the center, an open doorway led somewhere into darkness to the rear of the building. There were two bare wood tables and some straight-backed chairs, two of which had been toppled over. One table had been tipped to its side. Dust, old papers and cigar butts littered the floor. An empty bottle and several glasses stood on the counter. The opened entrance door obscured Taggert's vision on the left. Haldane urged him on, impatient, fretful. Outside, water dripped monotonously from the eaves. There was no other sound except Haldane's labored breathing. Abruptly coming to a decision, Taggert said again, "Come on, Major. I reckon it is all right."

They moved slowly across the threshold, Taggert aiding Haldane's uncertain steps. Carefully he closed the door behind him, then glanced to his left. Silence. Then, his quick intake of breath. "No," Taggert almost groaned, "it ain't all right, Major. I just plain walked you right into trouble."

At the far left end of the room, twenty feet away, six men stood facing him, all with leveled six-shooters. In the center of the group a bare-footed girl in faded calico strained against ropes binding her to a straight-backed chair. Long blonde hair hung in a tangled cascade from her lowered head. One man had a dirt-begrimed paw clamped over the girl's mouth; his other arm came tightly around her neck. Now he released his hold and Taggert heard the frantic gasping rush of air into the girl's lungs. A bulky-shouldered bewhiskered man behind the others nodded contemptuously. "Correct, Johnny Reb! You walked right into it." Sudden hoots of laughter rose from the group.

Taggert raised above his head the arm not supporting Haldane. He started to say something. Black Whiskers interrupted, "Get both those arms up, Reb! and lift 'em fast, too!"

"He's hurt bad," Taggert protested. "He can't be any risk to you."

Black Whiskers' eyes were like pale blue agate. He nodded shortly. "Come away from that door. Get over toward that back wall. Don't try to—"

"Ain't likely to," Taggert said reluctantly. He assisted Haldane across the floor, mind working fast. A murderous looking group, he was thinking, with their unshaven faces, shabby clothing, and leveled six-shooters.

One man snickered. "We been watching you ride through yonder window. You acted like you wa'n't sure of your welcome. Looked like you and your pard never would make up your minds. He appears took indisposed—"

Laughter and derogatory remarks filled the room. Taggert's hair bristled; his muscles tensed. With an effort he kept his head. Cautiously he reached to an overturned chair and lowered Haldane to its seat. The major, frowning, eyes not quite in focus, struggled to concentrate on what was taking place. Taggert said, level-voiced, "I reckon we can talk this over. My major, here, is bad wounded. He needs a doctor and—"

Black Whiskers cut in, "Nothing to talk over, Johnny Reb. We want your sidearms and your horses. We'll be taking them."

Taggert shrugged. "Take 'em by all means, gents. We don't aim to kick up any fuss. All's I want is to get my major to a bed—"

"He ain't going to need no bed," a hard-visaged man stated shortly. "Nor you, nuther,

14

Gray-Back." He had removed his hand from the girl's mouth and her head lifted a little, the long blonde hair tangled about her features, lined with despair. She didn't speak, just sagged against her ropes. Three other men shifted position. Back of them, sprawled on the floor, was a motionless gray-haired figure in civilian clothing. Coagulating blood stained the floor beneath the body. Taggert didn't need to be told that the gray-haired man was dead. He shifted his gaze to the others. At least one he'd seen before. A motley dirty group in ragtag uniforms, three Federal, two Confederate.

Black Whiskers said harshly, "Zeke called the turn, Reb. Neither of you will need beds again. After we've left, the girl can bury you—if she's able—" Taggert interrupted to point out that killing them wouldn't do any good, but Black Whiskers cut in, "It's no good, Reb. We couldn't risk having you identify us some day. That's the way it's got to be."

Haldane stirred in his chair, mind momentarily clear. Swaying to his feet, he exclaimed hotly, "Guerillas! Damned guerillas!"

"You're right, Major." Taggert spoke bitterly. "Guerilla bastuds!" He lowered Haldane back to the chair and raised his arms again, hands clasped atop his head. "Guerilla bastuds with no guts for fighting on either side. Just raiding when fighting men have passed."

15

Black Whiskers shrugged. "Guerillas? Sure. At least we know what we want, which is more than can be said of soldiers either of North or South. The majority are fighting either for Northern money men, or wealthy slave holders. Plain fools, the lot of you. Our way's safer."

Taggert's temper rose. "Guerillas! Murdering skunks, killing old people, robbing helpless folks, burning homes, attacking young girls—"

"Hush your tongue, Reb," Black Whiskers grated. His six-shooter lifted a trifle. "You already said too much."

Haldane spoke softly from behind Taggert, tones not reaching far. "Easy, Judd. These men hold the whip-hand. No need of riling them."

Black Whiskers said something to the man behind him. Others joined the conversation, and there was a lessening of watchfulness. Haldane spoke again. "Move fast when the time comes, Judd. Direct your fire to the left. I'll aim to the right. Keep your shots clear of the girl."

Taggert didn't turn his head. His lips scarcely moved. "Right, Major. I just hope our charges kept dry—"

Black Whiskers' voice interposed, mockingly, "Sorry to keep you waiting, gentlemen. It's been just a small matter of picking your executioners that occupied us. Nobody likes a Johnny Reb, and the same goes for blue-bellies and those Black Republicans that that baboon, Lincoln, foisted on this glorious section of God's good earth. And one other trifle has delayed your trial, gentlemen—" Taggert spat contemptuously. "A trial according to our lights," Black Whiskers nodded blandly. "You've already been tried. A sentence of execution has been passed. We have voted that you shall have one minute to indulge in prayers before departing to meet your Maker. A sort of preparation—"

The interruption, when it came, carried all the violent impact of an earth-shaking crash of thunderbolts. "No! This execution of which you speak, dog with the black whiskers, is not to be, now or at any time. I demand you put down those pistols. At once!"

The words were spoken in a rather unnatural voice, giving an impression the speaker was endeavoring to disguise the tones. An abrupt silence engulfed the big room. Heads, as though attached to a single swivel, jerked toward the doorway in the rear wall.

A single figure stood there, dominating the room like some dark Nemesis, a figure clothed in a long black cloak, slightly parted to reveal shirt and booted trouser legs of the same funereal hue. A broad-brimmed black felt hat was drawn low on the forehead, and a black silk handkerchief tied across the nose concealed all but the dark eyes, eyes that looked fully as dangerous as the pair of short-barreled derringer pistols extending in each fist toward the guerillas.

Consternation swept across Black Whiskers' scowling face. The guerillas, jaws agape, shifted uneasily. One guerilla's gun clattered to the floor. Another gasped, "Goddlemighty! Who's that?"

Taggert swung back from the black figure in the doorway, dropping his arms, reaching toward holster. Black Whiskers had already moved into action. Cursing, he leaped behind the nearest guerilla and, aiming over the man's shoulder, fired. Taggert's gun roared at the same moment. He felt the breeze of Black Whiskers' slug as it whined past his ear. The man in front of Black Whiskers plunged to the floor. There came the hot detonation of Haldane's gun.

Black Whiskers, followed by three guerillas, made a frantic rush for the door. One succeeded in jerking it open before he crashed down, allowing Black Whiskers and one other to plunge through to the gallery, firing as they ran. Heavy explosions shook the room. Dust sifted down from ancient rafters. Black powdersmoke swirled through the air. It was all a mad blur of running feet, shooting, cursing men. Haldane lurched up from his chair, staggered into Taggert, spoiling the sergeant's second shot, his own gun slipping from his fist to the floor.

A frustrated oath was torn from Haldane's throat. His right hand went to the saber at his side. It flashed smoothly from its scabbard.

Stumbling steps carried Haldane toward the open door where a guerilla paused, lifting his pistol. The saber glittered brightly as it swept through the air toward one side of the guerilla's neck. Taggert fired again. Then once more. He coughed acrid powdersmoke from his lungs.

Quite suddenly the room had gone quiet. Taggert leaped toward the doorway, only to go sprawling down as Haldane fell across his path. Cursing, Taggert clambered up and leaped outside. By the time he reached the gallery, two guerillas were mounted and spurring the horses savagely along the muddy road. Taggert steadied his gun barrel against a gallery upright, pulled trigger, missed. He swore savagely and tried again. This time the hammer fell with a dead clicking sound. The two riders disappeared around a bend in the road, the furiously driving hoofs of the horses flinging wet clods derisively toward the enraged Taggert. He shook one furious fist at them, then slowly turned back to the interior of the Boar & Tankard.

At first glance the floor seemed strewn with bodies. Four guerillas lay without movement, three near the elderly dead man they'd seen on arrival. Taggert's eyes went instantly to the still form of his major, above whom knelt the strange figure in the black mask, holding a flask to Haldane's lips. The major's face above matted tawny whiskers was the color of ashes.

The guerilla Haldane had sabered to death was crumpled a few feet off, and the girl with the blonde hair sat bound in her chair as before, struggling to make herself heard. Taggert said to the kneeling figure in the black mask, his words dull, lifeless, "Reckon it's too late for that, mister. My major's finished."

"What you say is of the utmost nonsense!" Briefly the dark mask lifted, eyes gleaming impatiently above black silk. "It is only that your major is exhausted, and he has fainted. But the wound is of much seriousness. See to the girl." The words were throaty, sounding not quite normal. It didn't occur to Taggert to ignore them.

For the moment he had forgotten the girl. By now some color had returned to her cheeks. Even then, Taggert was conscious of the slim length of bare leg and swelling breasts beneath faded calico. Carefully, he brushed back the girl's blonde hair, then drew his knife, opened it and set the girl free. She mumbled thanks, but Taggert had already swung back to Haldane. His jaw dropped in surprise. The stranger in black had vanished. Haldane was making feeble efforts to rise. The whisky flask had been left nearby. Taggert swung back to the girl, asking, "Where'd that feller in black go so fast?"

Intent on rubbing the numbness from rope-cramped limbs, she didn't reply at once. The girl's eyes were very blue, the color of cornflowers, when she raised them to his face. One arm lifted, brushed back a strand of blonde hair. "I could not say." The low-spoken words just reached Taggert.

"You mean you don't know?" he insisted.

She continued to rub one ankle and said again, "I could not say."

Taggert glanced around bewilderedly. He took quick steps toward the doorway leading to the rear of the building, followed a short way along a dark hall with closed doors on either side. Suddenly he paused, listening. Faintly to his ears came the sounds of a running horse, churning up gumbo mud. By the time Taggert had dashed back to the gallery, the sounds had vanished. There was no one to be seen on the muddy roadway. He returned to the big room. The blonde girl still sat massaging her wrists. Taggert knelt at Haldane's side, lifted the flask to the major's lips. Haldane coughed and his eyelids fluttered. He stared vacantly at Taggert a moment, gaze clearing. "Is—is it all right, Judd?"

"Better than it was, Major," Taggert conceded. "But we're set afoot. Two of them guerilla skunks got free on our hawsses."

CHAPTER 2

Later, Garth Haldane had but a brief memory of the following days and nights. For long there was only darkness, then sharp moments of excruciating pain, broken by bitter draughts of medicine, before oblivion again engulfed him. There were hot feverish hours and unslaked thirst, restless delirium, a burning torture in his shoulder. But there came a day finally when he awoke, clear-headed, though still weak, in a room he'd never before seen, to find himself stretched in a four-poster bed. Late afternoon sun flooded through a window to cast a bright rectangle on a threadbare carpet. There was an ancient walnut dresser and bureau, chairs, a washstand. A clothes stand held what was left of his shabby Confederate uniform. A closed door stood opposite the foot of the bed.

Haldane shifted slightly and winced at a twinge in his shoulder. To his amusement he discovered he was clothed in a voluminous nightshirt. He sank back to the pillow and wondered where Judd was. A moment later the door opened and he saw Taggert peer cautiously through. Haldane said in a weak voice, "Come along in, Judd. I'm not asleep."

Taggert came the rest of the way and dropped

into a chair. "Lord A'mighty, Major, it's good to hear your voice. You sound sort of puny though. Laure says I'm not to stay too long?"

"Laure?" Haldane frowned.

"The girl here's been 'tending you. Laure Gabriel. It was her that knew of this sawbones living off in the timber. She brought him." Haldane's frown deepened. "You saying you don't remember what happened."

"Not much. I do remember a girl when we arrived here—tied in a chair—guerillas. Hell, Judd, bring me up to date."

Taggert hunched his chair closer, a lean dark man with keen black eyes, showing some trace of Cherokee blood. His stained blouse was of 8th Texas Cavalry issue, with a wide gash in one arm. His patched and faded trousers, with yellow stripes, had been taken from the body of a dead Federal. His boots were cracked, the sole of one held in place by a length of knotted rawhide. He said, "So you've forgot Laure Gabriel. Think back a couple of years, almost. Missionary Ridge. Not far from there—"

"Ah, yes, I remember Missionary Ridge. Something like a third of the Rangers were lost there—"

"But we whupped them damn blue-bellies, didn't we? Then, right after, remember that little cabin where we rode in just in time to save Laure from another gang of guerillas, after they'd killed her maw and paw. This is the second time that big bastud with the black whiskers—I recognized him right off—has slipped through our fingers—" Taggert broke off, shook his head. "Damned if I can see how you'd forget her—that blonde hair and—and—"

"Apparently I have a poor memory for faces."

Taggert looked disgusted. "Maybe you mean girls. I recollect that time we went into rest quarters, down in Gawgia. All them Cave Springs ladies tryin' to please and make us to home, and all's you could do was bury your nose in a book. You didn't 'tend one dance or cake social."

Haldane smiled thinly. "All right, this is the same girl. What is she doing here?"

"After she was left alone down there, she come here to help her uncle with this Boar and Tankard Inn, which same has been here since Revolutionary days. It come down through the family to Laure's uncle. Before the Yanks got jealous of Texas and started a war against the whole South, this Boar and Tankard was right popular with cotton and tobacco growers hereabouts. They used to come and stay with their families and fish in a little old lake near here. I already caught me some perch—"

"Since when did you take up fishing?" Haldane looked amused. "I suppose, though, you had to pass time—"

"Pass time hell!" Taggert growled. "We was

24

hungry, didn't have nothing but some parched corn and a handful of corncake and some acorns to grind for cawfee. Laure says what the first Yanks that come through took didn't leave much for our forces to clean up when they come through. Then the blue-bellies again, then once more, Confeds. Lucky the war moved on. Last come guerillas, and what they had in mind— well, before that, that gang had been captured by Yanks and held prisoner. During that last battle you and me fought, the guerillas escaped afoot. So they cut across country and arrived here. Laure heard 'em talking over things before we arrived. They tortured and killed her uncle—her aunt died last year—'cause he wouldn't tell 'em where his money was hid, him not having any money to hide. Then they spied us comin'."

"I'm still not clear what happened that day. I seem to remember a man in a black mask—and then there was shooting. What became—?"

"Somethin' mighty odd about that hombre," Taggert scowled, "though I can't kick, 'cause he saved our lives. But he just sort of disappeared like. By Gawd, if I ever lay eyes on that big-bodied skunk with the black whiskers that got clean away!"

"Stick to your story, Judd. Couldn't you make out anything about that man with the black mask?"

"Nary a thing. I saw him feedin' you some

whisky, then he told me to go untie Laure. While I was disropin' her, he plumb took off. I could just see his eyes, sort of big and dark. He had something funny about his voice, like he was making it sound deeper than was natural. I did notice his hand on the liquor flask. Long white fingers, with an odd-lookin' ring on one of 'em. Heavy sort of stone, the color of beef suet with red blotches, with a sort of design cut in it—"

"What does the girl—this Laure—say about him?"

"I think Laure knows him. She always changes the subject when I get inquisitive. Just says she can't talk about it."

"Can't or won't?"

"Comes down to the same thing, don't it? She never does talk much. Seems sort of shy. But that night after the doctor was brought, I noticed she paid him with a gold-piece. Now where would a girl like Laure get gold these days? You know what? I think that feller in the black mask give it to her. And it wa'n't like no gold-piece I ever saw before. It had eight sides to it—"

"Likely California-minted. Gold, eh? Gold has been pretty scarce in the Confederacy."

"You figure that hombre in the black mask was a blue-belly? Hell, no Yank would have helped us."

"I'm not so sure, Judd. I figure the Yanks hate guerillas as much as we do. But enough of that. I

26

imagine Laure will be glad when we leave here. Should any Yanks catch her sheltering a pair of Texans—"

"Don't let that worry you. Miss Laure's got a heap of gratitude for saving her from the guerillas, and that's twice now—"

Haldane said, "The gratitude is on my side. I'm beholden to the girl, and the man in the black mask as well. I hope to be up in a few days. You've been fishing while I've been lazing here."

"Fishing? Just twice. For food. I've been scouting in and out around Bentonville. Made some sallies through the brush and pine—"

"Just what have you been up to, Judd?" Haldane looked curious.

Taggert didn't reply at once, then, "Look here, I'll bet you don't know yet that Gen'l Lee surrendered to Grant." And at Haldane's sharp glance, "It's true. We lost at Bentonville, then at some place called Appomattox they got Gen'l Lee in some sort of trap, probably an underhanded trick, and they got Ol' Bob to promise to let up a mite on the blue-bellies, but we'll get organized again and—"

"So the war's over," Haldane muttered half to himself.

" 'Course it ain't over," Taggert denied indignantly. "If the truth was knowed, us Texans really got the Yanks on the run. Gen'l Johnston ain't surrendered yet. And Gen'l Kirby Smith—"

But Garth Haldane had again fallen asleep. Taggert rose silently and tiptoed out of the room. That was one of a half-dozen of Taggert's widely spaced visits, about which he was very evasive under Haldane's questioning. Somewhere, Haldane gathered, Taggert had secured a mule and was making frequent trips to Bentonville. "Me, ridin' a mule," Taggert had said disgustedly. "Imagine a Texan on a mule." The fact remained that Taggert always returned from such forays with plentiful supplies of beans, bacon, flour, and other foodstuffs. It worried Haldane as to their source, though he didn't yet feel up to grilling Taggert. During one visit Haldane asked, "What sort of terms did Grant give General Lee?"

"Well, now, Major, suh, I ain't just sure, but I figure Ol' Bob put it up to Gen'l Useless that we wouldn't stand for no harsh treatment. As I got it, them that surrendered is allowed to go home, retainin' their sidearms and hawsses, if any, providin' they got a pay-role paper." Haldane asked what sort of parole paper was meant. "Nothin' to fret over," Taggert evaded. "I got us a couple." Under further questioning he admitted to having found a friend in Bentonville that fixed things.

"You mean such papers have been forged?"

Taggert squirmed. "How else could I get 'em, Major?"

Haldane frowned. "It doesn't sound honorable. Exactly what are they?"

"Honorable be damned! The paper says you got to swear allegiance to the U.S. states and not to take up arms against the North. If a man don't have a pay-role paper, he is judged to be a guerilla and shot on sight. It's certain you and me ain't surrendered, so we got to have them pay-role papers. Pretty soon we'll get our regiment re-formed and finish whuppin' them Yanks—"

Haldane said slowly, "Judged and shot as a guerilla. That sounds pretty harsh. Judd, get it through your head the war's over. I'm beginning to think about home. You remember word reached us that raiding Comanches burned White Hawk Acres and ran off cattle. There'll be a lot of rebuilding to do. We've got to get started back, Judd."

And that was the big problem: how to avoid surrendering, make their way back to Texas, across country, and commence the restoration of White Hawk Acres. All that with no money.

White Hawk Acres, the great white house with portico and tall pillars which Garth Haldane's father had raised on his holdings of considerable acreage, near San Antonio, where cotton, blooded horses and beef cattle had furnished a more than adequate income . . . And now, Garth Haldane considered, father and mother and one brother were no longer alive, and the big house had been burned to the ground. Now, only Garth remained to carry on the old family name and rebuild White Hawk.

Thus the thoughts coursing his mind as he rested in a rocking chair, bolstered with pillows, one afternoon on the rear porch of the Boar & Tankard Inn. He possessed a sense of well-being, though slightly fatigued from the short walk he'd taken that morning. The sun was bright on the oaks beyond the weathered outbuildings of the Inn. Fleecy clouds drifted across a serene sky. A redheaded woodpecker drew a swift arc of red, white, and black from a dogwood to a tall pine. It still seemed odd this feeling of peaceful solitude, after four years of thundering guns. Fingers strayed through his ragged beard. At any rate, his uniform was clean and patched once more, thanks to that girl—Laure?

A bit of color among the trees caught his eye and he saw Laure Gabriel approaching from a trip to the creek to gather water cress. An old straw bonnet covered the blonde hair; the faded calico was taut across the swelling breasts. The dress, stained wetly, came but a short distance below the bare knees and her bare feet shone with a sort of golden sheen along the sunlit path. A rather slatternly looking girl, Haldane thought, as he saw now she carried with the water cress an armful of wild iris, pale against the color of her cornflower-blue eyes.

She mounted the steps to the porch. "You feelin' all right, Major Haldane?" He admitted being a little weary from the exercise he'd taken that morning, remembering the girl's hand on his arm as they'd walked to the creek and back. "But I feel right good, Miss Laure. You must have waded deep to get that cress."

"Yes, suh, but it ain't fittin' Sergeant Taggert should furnish all our vittles, when I can help a mite." Haldane asked her a question. The girl evaded his eyes. "No, suh, I can't say how he works it to get so much sow-belly and sech." She started to pass, but Haldane detained her to ask if she knew when Taggert would next return. "I couldn't say, suh," the girl replied, and continued on into the Inn.

A scowl crossed Haldane's bewhiskered face. That girl never did appear to have an answer to any of his probing. A rather silent girl; in addition, a very pretty one. She apparently lacked education and breeding, but given an opportunity she would be lovely.

Once Haldane thought he heard hoofbeats. Ten minutes later he was certain, when he spied Judd Taggert emerging through the trees ringing the Inn buildings. Taggert carried a laden gunny sack. Behind him came a small-framed Negro, bearing a similar sack. Taggert spoke briefly to the man, who mounted the steps, rolled his eyes whitely at Haldane and passed on into the building. Taggert paused at Haldane's chair, his saturnine features brightening. "Dawg my eyes, Major, if you're not looking right perky. You look good." From a pocket he produced a bit of cornhusk and some tobacco crumbs, rolled a cigarette. A sulphur match was scratched on one thumbnail, flame touched to the cigarette. Blue smoke drifted on the soft spring breeze.

Haldane said dryly, "I see you've acquired a body servant, Judd."

"Huh?" Taggert rubbed his unshaven chin, then the hand holding the cigarette jerked toward the house. "Oh, him. He's been here before. You just never ain't seen him. He's a good worker, Major."

"I don't doubt it. Where'd you get him?"

"Over toward Bentonville way. Name's Candent—Lustrous Candent. He don't aim to be free, regardless what Lincoln proclamationed. Used to belong to Colonel Joel Candent. 'Member, used to raise cows up Austin way. A neighbor of ours, you might say . . . Well, Colonel Candent was killed down near Atlanta, last fall. Some Yanks picked Lustrous up, told him he was free and didn't have to work no more, and put him to work helpin' 'round that Bentonville supply depot they maintains there, workin' in the office. But nobody yet give him any wages and everybody bosses him. Him and me just got acquainted one night when I was scoutin' 'round the supply depot. We had to eat, didn't we—?"

Haldane frowned. "So now we're beholden to him. And he's been helping you steal food from the Yanks. How do you figure to pay him?"

32

Taggert stared. "Pay?"

"He is now considered a free man."

"War ain't over yet, Major. So long's we see no harm don't come to Lustrous and he eats regular, what more can he ask?"

Haldane sighed. "Judd, face the facts. Slavery is done for. We're not whipped, but we've gone as far as we can without the means, the money, and ammunition, to carry on a war. We've run out of man-power as well. Consider that last contingent that joined our infantry. Old men and boys armed with ancient flintlocks and shotguns, already in rags—"

"Them's Texans for you," Taggert said proudly. "They got guts."

"Texans get cold and hungry and die, just like other men, dammit! Dead men can't fight. It's still not clear in my mind what brought on all this madness. Father was never in favor of slavery, and planned to free our help as fast as possible. What in God's name were you fighting for? You didn't own slaves, long as you've been with our family. The majority of the South's fighting men never owned a slave in their lives, nor even a chance to purchase any. Just ask yourself—"

"Me, I ain't fighting for the South. I'm fighting for Texas and the Haldanes and White Hawk Acres. And now with Lincoln dead I figure we can get organized again—" He stopped at a look from Haldane, then went on, "Well, come right down to it, I ain't for slavery neither. There's a heap of difference between slavin' a man, and takin' him in and carin' for him. Maybe Lincoln had different ideas once, too. I remember readin' in the San 'Tonio *Alamo-Star* where Lincoln said, plain as the nose on a cow-critter's face, he didn't have no intention, directly or indirectly, to interfere with slavery where it existed. Remember?"

"I'm not likely to forget. I've a suspicion that Lincoln was a victim of political circumstances. What his crowd never did realize was that the South wasn't fighting to perpetuate slavery, but to run its life in its own way, without interference from the North. But when you get greedy, hot-headed men on both sides, war is inevitable." He added, "Quit thinking about *yesterday* and what used to be. We're going to head *west,* back to rebuild White Hawk and its herds, though God only knows where the money will come from—"

The rear door of the Inn opened and the Negro emerged, saying to Taggert, "Miss Laure say she don't want Ah should cut no moah fah wood right at de presen'. Got enuff, she say—"

Taggert cut him short with a nod. "This is him. Lustrous. They don't breed 'em no better than down Texas way. Now you take—"

"I get your point, Judd." Haldane looked at Lustrous, repressing a smile as he studied the man. He was very black, thin almost to the point of emaciation. About thirty years old, with a look of rawhide toughness. Atop the tightly kinked hair, fitting his skull like a cap, rested the blue, visored hat of a Union soldier. A patched, faded pair of Confederate trousers, sizes too large, bagged at the knees, held in place by a leather strap around the waist. The cavalry boots, cracked and patched, were run down at the heels. Beneath a Confederate artilleryman's blouse, with buttons missing, was a red undershirt. Haldane said, "I understand you're Lustrous Candent."

"Yassuh, Majuh, suh, at youah suhvice. Body suhvent to de late, lay-mented Cuhnel Candent."

Haldane nodded. "We'll find a way to repay you, Lustrous."

The man's head bobbed. "Ah ain't wuhhyin' 'bout no pay, suh. Ah's willin' to wuk foah y'all. All's Ah wants is to have me some white folks agin. An' lak de sahgent says—"

Taggert interposed hastily, "Lustrous, you'd best get along and see to them hawsses."

"Yassuh, Sahgent, Ah goes prompt." He turned and hurried off.

Haldane looked after him a moment, then, "What was this about horses, Judd? Have we acquired horses? If so, where?"

"And saddles." Taggert grinned. "I sort of liberated 'em from the Yanks, even done some brand-blottin' to change that U.S. brand to a sort

35

of White Hawk deesign. I been intendin' to tell you—"

"So now," Haldane said softly, "I'm beginning to understand where you got those parole papers—"

"Why not?" Taggert was unabashed. "There was Lustrous, with a free run of the depot and offices, and there was the pad of pay-role papers. It was him got 'em for me, and I did the right sort of scribbling on 'em. . . . I emancipated us a couple of guns, too—a Henry and a Spencer repeater. And ammunition for same. I figure we need the hawsses for ridin' west of that yesterday you mentioned." Now the sergeant began to look uneasy. "And we got two mules, too, one for packing and t'other for Lustrous to ride. And we can sort of ride trails that ain't too much traveled and get through to—"

"One minute, Judd," Haldane frowned. "Where does Lustrous figure to ride, and why—?"

Taggert looked miserable. "Well, you see it's this way, Major. He wants to get back to Texas and I promised him—"

Haldane exploded. "You promised to take him with us? Are you insane, Judd? We'll be traveling fast, avoiding Federal patrols. There may be fighting. We can't be burdened with him. I can't see—"

Taggert threw up his hands in resignation. "It was part of the bargain we made at that Yank

36

supply depot. For helping us get what we needed, I promised him he could go with us. All right, I'll just have to tell him the deal's off, but I sure hate to do it."

Slowly, Haldane shook his head. "You can't do that, Judd. You *promised*. I don't like it, but we'll take him, as you said."

Taggert brightened, sighing with relief. "So that's settled. It'll look better when you hit Texas to have a body servant, like you used to. Lustrous will take real good care of you, Major. Something else, he's got Colonel Candent's kit of razors and—"

Haldane snorted derisively. "Not a penny to my name and I need a body servant? You do have the damnedest ideas, Judd. All right, I'll take the hint. Tell him to bring those razors and get busy."

CHAPTER 3

The bright spring days approached summer. No longer was it necessary to aid Haldane's steps when he took his daily walk, though now he was commencing to miss the girl's presence. He had inspected the mules and horses in the pole corral Taggert had thrown up, back in the pines. Taggert and Lustrous Candent seemed forever busy checking the supplies they intended to take on the journey across country and in other ways preparing for the trip. But it was Laure who concerned Haldane now. He couldn't quite make up his mind about the girl. Once he had found her seated on the front gallery, an open book in her lap. She wore the same threadbare calico, over the bare feet and legs. The thick blonde hair was pinned carelessly about her head. The girl colored and hastily closed her book when he emerged on the gallery.

"I had no idea you could read—" Haldane commenced, then, lamely, "I mean I didn't realize you read"—pausing to pick up the small leatherbound volume and quickly scan the title—"*Lord Byron's Poems*." He replaced the book in her lap and brushed the bare, tanned arm in the movement.

"I jist tries to make out the letters, suh. Some

of them words is real pretty when you string 'em together." Haldane asked where she'd procured the book. She replied rather evasively, "I jist sort of picked it up, upstairs, and started in to studyin' of it. Some of the long words Sergeant Taggert explained to me."

For a brief instant the cornflower-blue eyes met his own innocently, but Haldane realized that a deeper intelligence lay there than he'd previously discerned. And for a second he gathered an absurd impression the girl was inwardly amused at something he had said or done. Feeling uncomfortable, he turned with no further word and strode back into the building. In the hall, leading to the rear, he muttered disdainfully, "Lord Byron's poetry. Silly, young girl stuff. Romanticism in a hinterlander. Still after four years of war, a bit of romance might be the saving of this country—anything to help people forget the needless slaughter. Perhaps I shouldn't ridicule the girl. If something could be done with that blonde hair, she'd be a beauty. And with proper gowns, stockings, slippers . . ." Impatiently he put the thought aside.

That night at supper, the blonde hair looked even less cared for. A smudge of soot darkened Laure Gabriel's cheek. Haldane and Taggert ate in silence the meal she'd prepared and served them before withdrawing to the kitchen. Taggert looked at him and chuckled. "You know, Major, you and Miss Laure should get better acquainted. She's a real nice girl, and pretty, too."

Haldane said stiffly, "Miss Laure and I get on very well."

Taggert chuckled. "You know, Garth, that girl does beat all. She's been reading poetry by some gaffer name of Byran or Byron. I been trying to teach her to read. First thing I knew she was recitin' whole lines, just from memory. A girl like her should ought to get an education. Now there ain't no finer schools than's to be found in Texas—"

Haldane loosed an oath. "Dammit, I don't want to hear any more of your ideas. It's bad enough we got to take Lustrous. You must be crazy if you think I'm going to take a girl along. We'll have mighty tough going before we make to cross the Mississippi. I can't put too much faith in those parole papers you got. Some Confed soldier that passed here yesterday told me some Texans had been stood against a well and shot because they lacked parole papers and had refused to surrender. The Yanks have patrols out to pick up such men—"

"You figuring to leave her here all alone? You know, I got a hunch she might have a sweetenin' on you, Major—"

Haldane upset a glass of water as he leaped up from the table. "Will you shut up?" Scowling, he left for the front gallery and proceeded to light one of the cigars Taggert had "emancipated" at the Yankee supply depot as he strode furiously back and forth along the rough gallery floor. The following morning when he awoke, Taggert had again disappeared. This time he was gone three days, though Lustrous remained at the Inn.

When Taggert did return he found Haldane down in the corral just unsaddling his horse. "You're riding again, Major!"

"I've been in the saddle every day since you left. What? Of course, I'm all right. Saddle muscles a mite lame, otherwise I'm ready to travel. I'll condition on the way. I've been thinking it over. Talked to a few soldiers heading home past here, about routes, Yank patrols, so on. We'll head as direct as possible down to New Orleans. Too many patrols checking the crossing farther north along the Mississippi. Sure, there'll be patrols at New Orleans, too, but we'll worry about that when we get there—" He broke off. "Where you been?"

Taggert lifted the saddle from the horse he'd been riding. "Been scourin' the country, Major. I knew you felt like I did about leaving Laure when we pulled out. Finally found a middle-aged couple, name of Pope, that the Yanks had burned out. Good folks. They'll be glad to come here and have a home while they look after Miss Laure. Say, Garth, you still mad at me?"

Haldane said gruffly, "Never really was, Judd.

You were right about the girl. We can't leave her here alone. Explain matters to her—about the Popes coming. You can do it better than I can. When will the Popes arrive?"

" 'Bout three days, I reckon. I told 'em you was eager to start."

"Fine. We'll leave the day after they get settled in."

The Pope couple arrived and were as pleased with Laure Gabriel as she was with them. The following morning, early, preparations were made for departure. Lustrous Candent and Taggert were seeing to loading supplies on one mule. Lustrous had trimmed Haldane's hair and shaved him once more, leaving only a tawny mustache on his upper lip. Haldane stood on the rear porch, appreciating that his uniform had been neatly mended and pressed, and now finding himself somewhat reluctant to leave. It seemed he owed so much to Laure Gabriel. Haldane drew smoke from a cigar, appreciating a mellowness long forgotten, and watched smoke veil lazily across the pines. Haldane's gaze shifted, and he caught sight of Laure Gabriel talking to Taggert a short distance off. The two had their heads bent over an open book.

A moment later, Laure re-entered the Inn, nodding to Haldane as she passed. Taggert approached a few steps behind the girl. "You know something, Garth. I was telling Miss Laure that you planned we should go by way of New Orleans, and she agrees that that way will be safer." Haldane's mouth dropped open in surprise. Taggert went on, "It's this way. Men without parole papers—and there's thousands of Texans wouldn't surrender—will be looking to cross the M'sippi where the river's narrow, and the Yank patrols will be sure to think of that. But N'Orleans has been in Union hands for about three years now. The place will be swarming with Feds. Laure says that's the obvious place for a man without a parole to avoid, and the Feds will be careless, so maybe we can fool 'em. And Miss Laure says when we get to N'Orleans, we should go to Mason Gallant's—"

"Who in the devil is Mason Gallant? And what does that girl know about New Orleans? Where does she get her information? First, she hardly talks at all, then all of a sudden she starts—"

"You got me, Garth. And that's the way that name sounded. Mason Gallant. Maybe that masked feller in black tipped her off."

"And that's all she knows?"

"That's all she'd say. Then she clammed up on me and left."

"It's all damned peculiar, Judd. Well, let's get started."

They gathered before the Inn, supplies and bundles lashed on to a mule named Pegasus.

The other mule, Hercules—both named by Lustrous—was to be the Negro's mount. Haldane was to ride a big chestnut gelding, Taggert, a wiry gray which still showed a healing brand burn, as did one of the mules. Laure and the two Popes stood on the gallery, waiting to say goodbye. Taggert and Lustrous climbed into saddles and waited impatiently. Haldane turned first to the Pope couple, shook their hands, while they promised to take good care of Laure. Looking at their lined, defeated faces, Haldane wondered if it wouldn't be the other way about.

He turned finally to Laure. The girl's blonde hair looked as untidy as ever, though there'd been some attempt to arrange it with a bit of soiled ribbon. But she looked clean, with a fine healthy sheen to her tanned skin. Color rose in her cheeks when she faced him, and the sole of one bare foot self-consciously rubbed against the instep of the other. He said, "Well, Miss Laure—" and hesitated.

Shyly she lifted the cornflower-blue eyes to meet his. "Well, suh—"

"Laure," Haldane swallowed hard, "I—I don't know how to thank you for all you've done. I'm under heavy obligation for your nursing and—well, everything. Someday, perhaps, when affairs have settled—"

Surprisingly she broke in, "That could be quite a spell, Majuh. The South ain't whupped yet—"

"Laure, Laure, you're as bad as Judd. Neither of you can realize the war's over."

"Ain't noways sure it is, Majuh, suh. But it's been a real pleasuah to have y'all heah. I ain't forget what I'm owin' you and the sahgent, nuther, for savin' me from them gurillas. There's nothin' owin' to me."

Haldane smiled, trying to keep his manner, tones, light. "You're a real lady, Laure Gabriel. So you figure you and I are quits, then?"

Slowly, smiling, Laure shook her head. "Somehow, Majuh, I don't cal'clate you'n me will evah be quits. I'll be thinkin' of you and, mebbe, you'll think of me, come an occasion . . ."

The blue eyes drew him on and he took her hand and started to lift it to his lips, then sensed, rather than heard, her low-spoken words. He bent his head, kissed her lightly on the lips. One warm young arm went about his neck. Their lips met a second time. Drawing apart, he felt strangely shaken and heard her say, "Take good care of yourself."

"And you the same." He tried to recapture the light mood. "Just you study hard on your Byron and you'll find other books, too. And so, it's farewell—"

She interposed, "Ah'm gittin' to know Mistah Load Byron real good, Majuh, suh," and then quoted in a rich measured tone holding no trace of her former method of speech:

"Farewell to thee . . . but when liberty rallies
"Once more in thy regions, remember me then . . ."

Haldane stared and again saw in the blue eyes that hidden something, but briefly revealed, divulging her secret amusement at a quality he couldn't quite comprehend. He turned abruptly away with no further good-byes, frowning perplexedly, muttering in amazement at his own feelings, and half stumbled down the gallery steps, conscious of the open-mouthed amazement of the Pope couple. He turned once and saw that Laure had already vanished within the building. He was still shaking his head, muttering, as he climbed into his saddle.

"I know just how it hits you, Garth," Taggert said unfeelingly. "She kissed me, too, just before you come out. Sort of shakes a man right down to his heel-taps, don't it?"

Haldane had no reply for that. He shoved his feet into stirrups. "All right, Judd. We're headed west at long last. Let's get riding."

They moved off, the men lifting their hats to Mrs. Pope, and made a turn on the pine-flanked road. Taggert scowled, "You know something, Garth? I got a hunch that Miss Laure knowed that Byron book, even before I helped her with the words."

Haldane replied fervently, "If she didn't know more than that Byron book, I'm sadly mistaken."

46

CHAPTER 4

The three men and mounts pushed steadily on toward the southwest, trying to avoid the main roads, choked with returning soldiers, making a hidden camp at night, while Lustrous exploited his culinary skill over small fires. Day after day there were the same dusty roads of granitic sand or clay, leading them across rolling plateaus, past undulating grass ridges and through deeply slashed valleys. When it rained, the going was choked with a tenacious gumbo. The scene varied little, the route bordered with tall pines, varied with oak and ash or walnut. At times the pike flowed evenly between wide fields of stubble, weed-grown, or past ruined plantations. And always on the road, wherever they went, they met men in blue, hurrying north; gray clad men heading south. Mostly on foot. Some had horses or mules; one man had been riding a cow. There were a few in wagons, the majority legless men, these. Scarred, mutilated, unshaven men with crutches and canes cut from tree limbs, and with empty sleeves pinned back to one shoulder.

They broiled in daily muggy heat. The flies were a torment. Each day brought its difficulties, and there were always rivers to cross; sometimes they detoured through a swamp. Seldom was there a bridge or small ferry; usually, they had to find shallow fording spots.

Taggert swore wrathfully. "S'help me I'm getting nightmares about rivers. Seems like we're no sooner dry from one than we're in another. We crossed the Great Peedee and the Lynches River and the Watersee and the Congaree where it run into Saluda near Columbia—" He scowled blackly. "No fresh supplies in Columbia—place half burned to the ground. From causes unknown, they said. Folks still wonderin' how the fire started, and any half-wit fool would know where Sherman passed, it was caused by bastud bluebellies."

With food scarce in a war-ravaged land, they'd been forced to rely on shooting wild turkey, squirrel or rabbit. They crossed the Savannah River boundary between South Carolina and Georgia and made camp in a tall stand of pine trees. While they were making camp, Haldane saw something glittering yellow, tumble from Lustrous's pocket. Haldane questioned him and, somewhat sheepishly, the man handed Haldane an octagonal gold-piece. Further questioning brought out the fact Laure Gabriel had given the money to Lustrous.

"But you wan't to have it yit," Lustrous explained earnestly. "Miss Laure tells me jist to give it you when you is in diah straits—them's her wo'ds—diah straits. She didn't want you should go hungry, Majuh, suh."

Haldane swallowed hard and walked off to be alone among the pine trees. Taggert followed a few minutes later. Taggert said, "Maybe them guerilla bastuds was on the right track after all, when they tortured Laure's uncle to make him say where his money was hid."

"I don't think so," Haldane said slowly. His eyes looked moist. "She couldn't have had much money. I don't like it, Judd. She needed it more than we do. As if I wasn't already under enough obligation—"

"Hell's bells, if she hadn't wanted you to have it, she wouldn't have give it to Lustrous for you. If you ain't blind, you'd know why she done it too."

"What do you mean?"

"To me it was plain as the nose on a cow-critter's face. Laure Gabriel was in love with you."

Haldane said "Bosh!" and then abruptly, "Let's head back and see what Lustrous is fixing to eat."

Steadily they pursued a southwesterly course. July was drawing to a muggy close by the time they'd placed to the rear the greater part of Georgia with its rusty-red streams and red clay roads—ravished Georgia where Sherman and his hordes, like a blight of locusts, had eaten a swath of desolation fifty miles wide. The country was

49

stripped bare of all save stone and brick chimneys rising dejectedly from ash-heaps. Fields had been burned over, stock destroyed. At one point an old wood-burning locomotive lay rusting on its side, and there were charred remnants of wooden box cars. Steel rails had been ripped from cross-ties, heated until red-hot and then twisted around telegraph poles, setting fire to poles and killing trees. Such twisted spirals of metal, Haldane said, were called Lincoln Neckties.

By the end of August, they negotiated the Chattahoochie River and entered Alabama. Two days after crossing into Alabama their rations had again run low; remaining were a scant inch from a slab of bacon, and a couple of handfuls of corn flour. Reaching a small lake—it was little more than a pond—enclosed by a thicket of willow and tupelo trees, they endeavored to catch a fish or two, but with no success. Disgruntled, they consumed the remaining food and decided to camp there for the night. They spread their blankets on a slope of wild verbena crowned with a clump of tulip poplars.

Twilight had scarcely vanished when hoofbeats sounded along the road leading to the lake. Glancing down the long slope, Haldane made out through the gathering gloom, a group of some thirty blue-clad Federal cavalrymen in the vanguard of a supply wagon drawn by mules. Haldane whispered it would be better to remain where they were, hidden in the trees, until the soldiers passed on.

The difficulty rose when they failed to pass on, but instead, dismounted and made camp not far from the shore of the lake. The night deepened; stars burned overhead. Haldane, Taggert, and Lustrous lay on their stomachs peering down the slope where small fires winked into view. The minutes passed. Taggert stirred hungrily. "I smell coffee."

Haldane whispered, "Judd, do you suppose they'd give us a cup if we went down and surrendered?"

Taggert chuckled. "Terry's Rangers used to do better than that. We could try, Garth. I'm gettin' tired of tightening my belt all the time." With more conversation, a plan took concrete form. Lustrous was included in the plan and his part made clear to him. None of the three men moved, until the fires below had burned low and the weary cavalrymen had rolled into blankets. Haldane noted they hadn't even bothered to post a sentry.

An hour passed before he gave the word to move. Silently, the three moved down the slope, leading behind two horses and the mules. Ten minutes later they had merged with the trees and brush surrounding the lake. The sleeping Federals could be seen more clearly now in the light of a single fire still burning.

The surprise came as a hideous awakening to the Union cavalrymen. From two sides of them came sudden shots from Henry and Spencer rifles. Shrill rebel yells ripped violently through the peaceful night. Back in the brush, Lustrous kicked up considerable fuss, driving mules and horses, here and there. There came more firing, this time from different points. Leaden slugs winged angrily through the air. Thudding hoofs tore through the brush, first at one side, then another. There came more yelling and exultant cries.

The aroused cavalrymen were out of blankets now, gazing stupidly about. Some of them had difficulty locating their arms. Several dashed frantically for the shelter of the supply wagon. More shooting crashed from the brush. A handful of soldiers seized carbines, but were too upset by the sudden attack to know where to aim, when no enemy was in view.

Haldane's stern tones rang suddenly from the thicket. "You're my prisoners! I advise you to surrender without further opposition. Drop guns! Lift arms in air! Be quick about it!"

A majority of arms shot skyward. Weapons clattered earthward. A single shot from a Spencer rifle whined through the camp, persuading certain recalcitrant ones. One of the men, a lieutenant, called a sharp order. There was no further resistance, if resistance it could be called.

Haldane again raised his voice. "Cease firing, men! They've surrendered." Exultant rebel yells greeted the words, coming from various points around the lake. Haldane called sharply for silence and supplemented the words with orders to imaginary officers. A minute later he strode into the Union camp, very tall and soldierly, unarmed except for his cap-and-ball pistol and the saber at his side. He halted within the small circle of firelight. "Who's the officer in command, here?" he demanded. "Speak fast, or else—"

A young lieutenant in shirt, underwear, and sockfeet introduced himself as James Faunce. Haldane acknowledged the introduction, giving his own name and rank with military formality. He saw at once, inwardly amused, that Faunce was bewildered and uneasy; he was callow, practically beardless. Haldane demanded certain information. Sulkily, the lieutenant refused to reply. Haldane spat caustic words, reminding Faunce that he and his men were prisoners, completely surrounded. Did Faunce wish him to order a renewed fire?

Lieutenant Faunce broke down. He was leading a detachment out of Mobile, to apprehend such Confederate troops as had refused to surrender. It was understood there were many such traveling through the South, especially men from Texas. That, Haldane told him, was a complete understatement. "Many" was no word to describe the number. He laughed sarcastically.

"That situation will change, Major Haldane." Faunce displayed a momentary belligerency. There were countless detachments like his scouring the country for Confederates who couldn't produce parole papers. Suddenly indignant, Faunce exclaimed, "This is an outrage! The war is over. You and I, sir, should be at peace—"

Curtly, Haldane interrupted to point out it was ridiculous to term hostilities at an end so long as an enemy declined to surrender. Wasn't Faunce aware, Haldane demanded with a convincing expression of surprise, that Texans never surrendered, that *their* part in the war, at least, was continuing, and that already Federal troops were retreating on several fronts, where a large Southern army had made a surprise landing across the Mississippi?

Faunce's jaw sagged; he was momentarily speechless. He finally blurted out he couldn't be expected to know all this. He and his men had been out of touch with headquarters for two weeks. "It must be true then—" Suddenly he checked the words. Haldane insisted on knowing to what Faunce referred. Reluctantly, Faunce said, "It was rumored your General Shelby and his Missouri troops, with thousands of Confederates, had escaped into Mexico at Eagle Pass, and is forming a coalition with Mexico's

Emperor Maximilian, to move against the United States."

Haldane's heart beat faster at the news, though he kept his voice contemptuous. "It's no idle rumor, Lieutenant, as your generals will soon learn, to their dismay."

"I doubt it," Faunce said angrily. "General Sherman has already been ordered to Texas to forestall such plans."

Haldane smiled coldly, stating carelessly (and untruthfully) that was indeed stale news. Hadn't the lieutenant heard that General Sherman and his troops were known to have bogged down in attempting a crossing of the Rio Grande, and had, in fact, been already annihilated? Faunce swallowed the tale whole. His face paled. Exclamations of consternation broke from his men. "So hostilities have again broken out," he conceded dismally, adding with sudden heat, "Your Jeff Davis should be hung for treason, instead of furthering the ambitions of Napoleon III and Maximilian in Mexico. Such procedure is a direct violation of the Monroe Doctrine."

That, Haldane stated tersely, was neither here nor there. "The point is, Lieutenant, you and your men pose a problem for me. We have orders to proceed at all speed. We do not wish to be burdened with prisoners. That leaves me no alternative."

Faunce jumped to conclusions. "Surely, you'll

not order an execution of prisoners, Major Haldane, men who have surrendered peacefully to you—why, why—that would be barbarous—"

Haldane whirled suddenly toward the trees, raising his voice. "Silence in the ranks back there! Captain Taggert, control your men! Lieutenant Candent, I want to hear no more of such threats. Have sergeants Hercules and Pegasus deploy their men to better advantage and prepare for action!"

Horses, mules, and men moved noisily in the brush. There came a couple of rebel yells, followed by a sharp reprimand in Taggert's harsh tones. The Union troopers glanced about uneasily.

Haldane swung back to Faunce, smiling thinly. "Do I understand you're prepared to resist, Lieutenant? Against overwhelming odds? And with gun barrels covering every man in your outfit? Hah! You speak nonsense, Lieutenant Faunce."

A quick glance toward the surrounding thicket convinced the imaginative Faunce that he had actually caught the glint of firelight on several gun barrels. He started to speak, but words stuck in his throat. The Federals shifted uneasily. Nervously, a sergeant suggested Faunce make some sort of terms. Faunce commended the suggestion and waited for Haldane to speak.

Haldane mentioned a certain plan that had occurred to him. He smiled pleasantly, spoke of the courtesies due an enemy; he didn't hold with harsh treatment of prisoners. "In short," he concluded, "I'll be willing to accept the parole of you and your men, Lieutenant, on condition you and your troopers continue to travel north, toward Tennessee, and surrender yourselves to the first Confederate force with which you come in contact. Otherwise . . ." Haldane shrugged regretfully, allowing an ominous thought to form in Faunce's imagination.

Faunce accepted the plan, though a bit stiffly, stating that Haldane could assure himself of complete cooperation. Haldane nodded carelessly and continued. There were conditions. It would be necessary for Faunce and his men to leave behind all arms, supplies and animals. The actual surrendering to Confederate forces, Haldane would be pleased to leave to Faunce's sense of honor at the first opportunity.

"On second thought," Haldane went on, "to expedite the actual act of surrender, I'm inclined to allow you to retain your horses. I do not wish to work a hardship on men unaccustomed to walking."

Faunce and his men brightened. The conditions were accepted with alacrity. The Yanks, none seasoned veterans, sighed with relief and rushed to get into clothing and roll blankets. Men hurried to unload supplies from the wagon, when Haldane, generously, suggested they keep the bulk of the food. Guns were dropped, sabers clanked to the earth, as the Federals hurried to mount. A driver climbed to the wagon, after rushing the mules into harness. Faunce offered a stiff salute, then brought his hand down before completing it. Haldane was already turning away. The lieutenant spoke from his saddle. "You have my thanks for very generous treatment, Major Haldane."

Haldane swung back, saying courteously, "Thank you. I think we both realize all Yanks and Johnny Rebs aren't as black as they're painted." He bowed and lifted one hand to hat brim. "And now, you'd best get moving. My men grow impatient." He raised his voice to issue a command to hidden men in the brush, "Watch closely, men. At first sign of any Fed rider turning back, jerk your triggers!"

There came the sudden concerted rush of horses' hoofs. The mules flung themselves into the traces, nearly overturning the supply wagon as one wheel careened crazily from an outcropping of limestone. Two minutes later, Faunce and his men having cut a wide swath through the brush, were rounding the first turn on the distant pike, churning up dust in the light of the rising moon. Haldane turned away to see the grinning faces of Taggert and Lustrous emerging from the brush.

"You really carried out the bluff in fine shape, fellows. Now, there's supplies. We'll really eat tonight." The words were lost in wild peals of laughter.

CHAPTER 5

The following dawn again found them on their way. Day followed day as the load on the pack-mule rapidly diminished. The terrain flattened out. Brown roads twisted between sedge fields, elbowed their way around swamps or passed deserted cotton-gins. Blackened cotton stalks in long neglected fields brought a sense of depression until their vision next fell on some grassy hillock, or their nostrils at evening caught the full fragrance of wild honeysuckle. The occasions were infrequent when they saw a cottonfield with Negroes, now free and being paid for labor, working to help an owner frantically trying to recover the lost fruits of four barren years.

Small streams became numerous. Nearing the southwest section of Alabama, the thick, oppressive heat was tempered by daily winds from the Gulf of Mexico. Thunderstorms became frequent; their clothing, either from perspiration or rain, was rarely dry. Lustrous became ill, and at the next town they entered they could find only a drunken horse doctor who fed them and prescribed scuppernong wine and sleep for the fever. Surprisingly the "medicine" worked and Lustrous was himself the following morning when they again mounted.

Early in September they crossed into Mississippi, passing through groves of live oaks and magnolias. The sandy roads were flanked continually with a tangle of blackberry vine, yellow jasmine, and Cherokee roses. They paused at a tiny settlement to read the placard tacked to the wall of an abandoned store, calling their attention to the fact that all unparoled Confederate military personnel was commanded to at once surrender to the nearest United States authorities. The penalty for failing to comply was instant execution upon capture. From then on they took a meandering route that took roads into small consideration, veering south to follow the coast line. Twice they came within distant view of the white sand beaches of Mississippi Sound, the number of small bays making them head for a time in a northwest direction.

Now the Pearl River, boundary between Mississippi and Louisiana lay ahead. They began to consider New Orleans. That, it appeared, bothered Taggert not at all. "Nope, Garth, I don't figure our uniforms will attract any notice a-tall. You and me will just take a *pasear* into the Federal Provost-Marshal's office, bold as brass, throw down your pay-role papers and demand transportation 'cross the Mississippi. It's my understandin' the Yank sunzabitches is obligated to furnish such transportation. I'm bettin' a plugged *peso* our pay-roles will pass 'thout question."

"I'm not so sure, Judd."

"Hah! You think them Yank bastuds won't be powerful anxious to get shet of a couple Texans? In another month, Garth, I figger you and me will be starting cow-critters outten the brush at White Hawk and slappin' hot brand on 'em."

The following day they emerged through a short range of low hills darted sparsely with shortleaf conifer and blackgum trees, then as the terrain leveled again, they experienced the torrid sun of open country. An hour later they reached an expanse of wet pine flats and were forced to slow pace while seeking more solid footing, thus avoiding numerous pools reflecting the brown trunks of surrounding trees, which in turn gave way to marshy swamplands and sluggish streams choked with water hyacinth. They avoided the northern shores of Lake Pontchartrain, skirting widely in hope of finding secure footing for their mounts, but found they were forced continually to deviate to evade lifeless estuaries surfaced with green scum.

Ancient cypress trees, boughs festooned with hanging strands of gray moss, like the beards of venerable grandfathers, reared above on either side, the huge trunks dripping, and exposed roots traveling horizontally along marshy earth, or below the surface of fetid waters. The growth became more profuse; Haldane and his companions found themselves in a seemingly impenetrable jungle of trees and twisting vines that clung and climbed and tangled the hoofs of animals. Now they were no longer even sure of their direction. They followed a narrow bayou for three miles and came upon the rotting remains of an old plank road which brought them once more to open country.

That cheering discovery was short-lived; the planks abruptly ceased. The earth beyond seemed firm though it gave off a distinct trembling impression beneath the hoofs of the animals, the hoofs making sucking sounds at each step. The men were drenched in perspiration. A region of bearded cypress lay ahead and for a brief time they were glad to escape to the shadowed depths. Then great gray swarms of mosquitoes formed a dense cloud about them. It was impossible to see the sky now. A moist green half-twilight showed the way through winding tunnels of water oak and cypress. Horses and mules splashed through slimy water, climbed to firmer footing, only to sink deeper at the next step. A malarial mist rose from the swamp waters.

The gray silence deepened. It became too dark to travel farther. They made a wet camp on a hummock. Horses and men were miserable. It was almost impossible to build a fire. A broken, rotting cypress limb, punky with decay, finally began to give off smoke. Cautiously the men added a bit of grass which, when dry, gave off a tiny flame though there was far more smoke than fire. They ate some stale biscuits, cold fried ham and a crumbling square of cornbread. The animals cropped disconsolately at coarse salty marsh grass. Mosquitoes attacked viciously, penetrating the blankets drawn over heads. Smoke from the rotting cypress limb stung their eyes; sweat seeped into their clothing. Hot muggy darkness enveloped them.

Haldane and his companions were saddled and away the instant it was light enough to travel, but it was close to nine o'clock before the greenish half-light assumed a more yellow hue. A half hour later they emerged in sunlight to find a roadway of crushed shell reaching diagonally across their path. They turned the mounts thankfully to the road which flashed, gleaming whitely, beneath a torrid sun, straight through marsh and cypress swamps, the cypresses giving way to moss-hung live-oak trees and undulating grass land with a bayou at one side.

Small shanties began to appear, having the aspect of Negro cabins. There was no sign of life about them. They may have been fishing or trappers' shanties. The road curved slightly to avoid a grove of live oaks and then again bisected a wide expanse of wet swampland. Taggert spoke suddenly, "Garth, up ahead there. What you make of it?"

Haldane narrowed his eyes against the light

reflecting from the water. At first there was just the shimmering glare, then, "If it didn't sound crazy I'd say it was a team hauling a boat through that swamp. But a queer-looking boat."

"It's a queer country," Taggert grunted. "Maybe they travel that way, hereabouts. Such places as there's footing, the team pulls the boat. If it gets too deep, the hawsses get in and ride— no, Garth, that ain't a boat. It's some sort of carriage."

They drew nearer and were able to see the vehicle more clearly. It was an open barouche with two occupants, one a grizzled Negro on the driver's seat. A pair of black horses harnessed to the carriage, struggled in water two feet deep, and with much splashing made futile efforts to extricate the vehicle, one corner of which stood very low, the left rear wheel hub being below the surface. Finally the lathered team quit, almost exhausted, heads hanging. The whip in the driver's hand dropped helplessly. A quantity of broken reeds strewn on the water, attested the prolonged exertions of the team.

Haldane and Taggert spurred ahead, leaving Lustrous and the mule to catch up. Haldane now saw the occupant in the rear seat was a woman. The driver was in rusty black and wore a scuffed silk hat. "That rig is sure bogged down," Taggert commented. "Now how in Gawd's name did they ever get so far off'n the pike?"

They drew nearer and Haldane saw the woman was clothed in a bodiced dress of gray, with full skirt and small bonnet of braided horsehair, trimmed within the brim with tiny white rosebuds. Immediately he became conscious of his own shabby appearance: the patches of dried mud plastered on mosquito welts; the stubble of tawny beard, ragged mustache; his faded gray uniform trousers, sweat-streaked shirt and worn boots. Guiding his horse to the shoulder of the shell road he lifted the battered slouch hat. "May we be of assistance . . . ?"

"It is assistance of the most urgent we require, M'sieu." She possessed a certain vivacity of manner; her speech was rapid, the phrasing, accent, with its dainty transpositions of *th* and *s* sounds to something verging on *z*'s was definitely French, and made a sort of music in Haldane's ears, so long unaccustomed to a feminine voice. Even at this distance he saw she had very white teeth and magnificent dark, long-lashed eyes. Hair that shone like a ripe chestnut was coiffured in a heavy knob at her nape; a fringe of bangs lay evenly along her forehead. A definite air of elegance hovered about her.

Wry humor tinged her tones. "These so stupid horses! It is that they feel of the oats wild, with a running of such swiftness that Boaz lost all of control." She gave Haldane to understand she had been enjoying a morning drive. The horses had taken the bit in their teeth, had—"made a running away of much furiousness and, *voici!*, we find ourselves in a predicament." Gestures of white hands embellished the story. The grizzled Negro driver listened with slack jaw.

Again, Haldane lifted his hat. "If I may be permitted to introduce myself—Major Garth Haldane, at your service." He heard her reply, ". . . Mme. Achille Galante," thinking, *So she has a husband,* even while introducing Taggert. Taggert acknowledged the words with a short nod, battered hat scarcely leaving his head, *en passant*, as he reined his mount into the water and grasped the left rear wheel of the barouche. He tugged, then announced to Haldane. "It's caught on something under the surface. We got to lift it loose." With no consideration for Mme. Galante's susceptibilities, he made blunt suggestions.

Haldane's cheeks reddened, but he saw the lady was smiling, apparently finding no flaw in Taggert's plan. Haldane guided his horse into the water and was immediately overcome with a feeling of helplessness. Then he saw her rise gracefully from the cushion and lean toward him. Awkwardly he extended his arms, then hesitated, lowering his eyes. On the floor of the barouche were a leather valise and a field-hand's wide-brimmed straw hat. While wondering to whom it belonged, the woman's voice interrupted, "With your permission, M'sieu."

Haldane didn't realize exactly how it was accomplished when he found her in his arms, his left supporting her shoulders, the right encircling her thighs in the gray dress. There was mischievous laughter in her eyes, and a faint dusting of freckles across the small nose. Unconsciously, he tightened his hold, feeling her breasts firm against his chest, sensing in a bemused way the vitality and feminine fragrance emanating from the rounded form he held so closely.

Her voice recalled him to reality. "This that we do, M'sieu, the Major, is most enjoyable, but are you certain the moment is a correct one?" Face crimson, he reined the horse back to the shell road, where she slipped lightly to earth.

Haldane saw now that Taggert had taken the driver, Boaz, behind him on his horse. Lustrous had arrived, and with the three men working together they managed to extricate the barouche's wheel from whatever had snagged it beneath the surface. The carriage righted itself and Taggert led the team back to the road, slimy mud dropping from the spokes as the marsh grudgingly surrendered its prey. Haldane dropped from his saddle to assist Mme. Galante to her seat. Boaz had already climbed up and, whip in hand, sat waiting. For some reason he appeared uneasy.

Mme. Galante extended a slim hand in a glove of gray net, saying, "At the moment, Major

Haldane, Sergeant Taggert, I do not try to make a proper expression of gratitude. You will pause a time in New Orleans, *n'est-ce pas*?"

Haldane told her they expected to stop in New Orleans but briefly on their way to Texas, until proper transportation across the river could be arranged. Thoughtfully, Mme. Galante pursed her full red lips. She pointed out certain difficulties demanding consideration. The city was terribly crowded; thousands of the military were passing through or stationed there permanently. Quarters would be extremely scarce; the St. Charles, the St. Louis Hotels had been commandeered by the Federal Military—"*cochons*!" Haldane shrugged and guessed they would make out all right.

"*Mais oui!*" Mme. Galante showed surprise that they couldn't comprehend matters were already arranged. "It will provide much pleasure to have you stay at our establishment, until your matters go forward." That, Haldane protested, was too great an imposition. His words were ruthlessly brushed aside with Gallic vivacity. Did not M'sieu, the Major, realize *soldats* of the Confederacy received something less than courteous treatment from U.S. officials. Further, it would be discreet to enter the city from the north; to the south and west would be encountered Federal patrols, searching for men in gray who had refused to surrender. Once within the city, the risk of such trouble lessened.

Smiling, Haldane remarked that she appeared to know a great deal regarding Federal movements. She replied that when pigs enter a dwelling it is wise to know where they root. "*Zut!* All this makes too much of talk. It is arranged. You and your men will take yourselves to the Maison Galante, on Rue Dauphine, when we depart." She failed to notice Haldane's start of surprise, while she was giving implicit directions. "I trust you will have no trouble."

It appeared that the matter was settled. She spoke briefly in French to Boaz, nodded, smiling, to Haldane and Taggert, and the carriage rolled swiftly away along the white shell road. Haldane said, "Well, there's your 'Mason Gallant,' Judd— the place, or man, Miss Laure mentioned."

Taggert nodded. "Something else, did you notice that ring she wore?" Haldane shook his head. Taggert scowled, "I could see it right through her lace glove. Remember I mentioned a ring worn by that masked man in black? Well, it was the same kind of ring. Do you reckon that members of some sort of secret organization wear such rings?" Haldane conceded the point. Taggert continued, "I don't swallow that talk of the team runnin' away, neither. Ain't no team goin' to plunge into the water and then turn, facing the road." He gestured toward a low-lying cypress ridge across the expanse of swamp water. "They must have come from yonderly—"

"Judd, the lady informed us she was out for a pleasure drive. Why should they go driving through a swamp—?"

"Exactly the point, Garth. Why in Gawd's name must you always take what a woman tells you for gospel truth? What was that man's hat doing in the barouche? And the valise? Now don't try to tell me she packed a picnic lunch in it. Maybe that hat belonged to her husband and they brought him out here to drown him, like you drown pups when you get too many in a litter."

"I can't believe it is the sort of hat Monsieur Galante would wear," Haldane frowned.

"Garth, you're improving fast," Taggert observed. "I used to maintain you knew nothing of women. Now, seems like, all you have to do is hold 'em in your arms, and you can tell what sort of hat the husband wears. Maybe if you're smart, you go a mite farther and learn her husband's whereabouts at any given minute—" Haldane cut him short with the suggestion they get riding again toward New Orleans.

They entered the outskirts, passing houses of stuccoed brick and cypress wood construction. Eventually they learned they were on Esplanade Street. Somehow, they'd missed Dauphine. On their way they'd passed a detachment of blue-clad Federals who paid them no attention. A short time later they'd halted on the docks facing the broad rolling river. The Mississippi surged full and golden beneath bright sunlight. A veritable forest of masts, smokestacks and funnels rose from massed, paint-chipped hulls along the water front. The wharves were crowded with soldiers, Negro and white, in blue uniforms. Townspeople, roustabouts, ancient colored women in patterned bandannas, pushed and jostled. Men, beyond military age, in seersucker and linen, white broad planters' hats and white trousers, lounged listlessly against the façades of buildings. A fish peddler guided a sagging wagon, crying loudly the virtues of his shrimps and frog-legs. A fishy river smell blended with a breeze from the swamps. There was a continuous babel of voices, Negro and Creole being almost submerged in the harsh accents of the North.

A certain arrogance dominated the features of Federals and some Negroes, among the latter a number of Negro policemen, self-important in their new authority. At the foot of Canal Street a group of Confederates were filing aboard a stern-wheeler, the *Ouachita Princess*. Out on the broad expanse of water, the twin-stacks of a side-wheeler made a wide smudge of black smoke, nearly obscuring a flat-boat with long sweeps, wallowing in its wake. More Federals rode past. New Orleans offered the appearance customary to an occupied city: there was much refuse scattered about; an air of neglect was in evidence. People

shuffled listlessly along the brick sidewalks—
banquettes, New Orleans called them.

The men rode north into Royal Street, horses'
hoofs clattering loudly over the stone paving
blocks, imported as ballast from Belgium, over
a century before. On either side, flush with the
street line, rose two- and three-storied stuccoed
brick buildings, with elaborately wrought, iron
railings along the upper galleries. Shuttered
dwellings mingled with shops in this district.
Negroes and whites thronged brick *banquettes*.
Haldane and his men passed to the rear of
St. Louis Cathedral, its three spires etched
sharply against the blue sky. Farther on, Haldane
told Lustrous to ask directions of a chimney-
sweep seated on the *banquette*, back resting
against a wall, his rope, palmetto and broom
straw heaped at his side.

They followed the sweep's directions, turned
into another street where a group of white men,
guarded by Federals, were cleaning refuse from
the cypress-lined gutters draining the street. Most
of the men wore shabby Confederate uniforms.
The men averted their faces grimly, and finally
learned they were on Ursulines Street, then made
another turning, Haldane suddenly conscious of
a growing strain and weariness. A few minutes
later they reached their destination on Dauphine
Street. It was a high, two-story structure, its
façade rising abruptly from the edge of the

banquette, its slate mansard roof, beneath tall chimneys, rising above its one-story neighbors. Bits of its plastered ivory-yellow wall surface had fallen away to show faded brick beneath. Along the street wall were four tall windows, at present green-shuttered. Between the two center windows was a wide arched entrance with a closed pair of iron-bound weathered oak doors. At the second floor a roofed balcony with an ornate grapevine design dominated the black wrought-iron railing.

There appeared no sign of life about the place. Lustrous was sent to make inquiries. The first sound of a heavy lion-head bronze knocker brought instant response in the form of a Negro servant in an apron; there ensued a brief discussion. Lustrous returned, grinning whitely. "Dey say we's expected and to lose no time interin'."

Haldane viewed through the arch of a short tunnel, the width to admit a carriage, and roofed overhead with cypress beams, an inviting vista of wide, flagstoned courtyard, deep shadows and flowering shrubs. His horse moved across the uneven brick pavement, with Haldane and Lustrous behind. The Maison Galante was constructed in the form of a hollow square. On four sides stairways of mahogany, with white painted banisters, rose to a roofed balcony. Open doorways on the first floor led, Haldane surmised, to servants' quarters and kitchen. The arched gates swung to behind them as he stepped stiffly down from his saddle, eyes seeking Mme. Galante. She was nowhere in sight, but a number of Negro servants gathered around. An ancient colored man in neat linen gave orders in English and French. Haldane gathered that horses and mules were to be taken to a livery two ilets (squares) distant. Baggage was gathered and Haldane was escorted to the gallery above, and thence to a tall, jalousied door which was thrust open before him. Glancing back, he saw Taggert entering an adjoining room. Lustrous had remained below with the other Negroes.

Haldane glanced about the high-ceilinged room, with its pair of draped fan windows. At one corner stood a four-poster bed covered with a mosquito *baire*. There was an armoire, a wash table, three rosewood chairs with worn beige upholstery. A pier glass was flanked on either side with watercolors in narrow frames. A small rosewood table held a pair of Sheffield candlesticks and a few books. There was a fireplace with brass screen. A reed rug covered the floor of polished cypress and in the center of the rug stood, incongruously, a huge round tub of cypress staves. The servant who had delivered Haldane's personal luggage was replaced by a second colored man, a short wizened fellow bearing towels. Apparently, Lustrous had been consulted: the new servant whipped from his pocket the kit of razors. Steamy basins of water and lather had been brought. Haldane stripped and sat in one of the chairs. Scissors and comb moved deftly through his thick tawny hair. Before the shaving was completed, a line of servants began entering, each bringing hot water which was emptied into the cypress tub.

Later, as he soaked weariness from his bones, Haldane saw that his uniform had been removed and fresh raiment left in its place. The contents of his pockets were arranged neatly on a table. By the time Haldane had got himself into an unaccustomed suit of some washable material, still another servant arrived, carrying a decanter, glasses, and a quantity of pale brown cigars in moist wrappers. The ancient colored man in charge of the servants, returned as Haldane was savoring the rare old bourbon. The Negro—his name was Robert—brought Mme. Galante's respects. She hoped the major was doing well. She would be pleased to receive him when he was thoroughly rested.

Haldane gave Robert the message he was doing far better than he had done in a number of years, adding his most grateful thanks. He'd be honored to pay Mme. Galante his respects at her convenience. He mentioned Achille Galante. Robert looked dubious but imparted the information that Monsieur Galante was presently in Paris. He bowed and stated food would arrive directly. As he departed, Haldane glanced through the doorway and saw that the sun was down; twilight had taken over. He turned back and lighted the candles in holders. Taggert entered, a suit like Haldane's hanging loosely on his rawboned frame. Grinning widely he said, "What do you make of it, Garth?"

Haldane smiled. "I seem to have a vague memory that someone thought the Provost-Marshal might be induced to extend charity to Confederates."

"Aw, you go to hell." He gestured toward the decanter. "Prime stuff, with authority. I already had three slugs and don't dast drink more until I get some food." Haldane expressed concern about Lustrous. "Don't you fret about him, Garth. I spied him a mite back, sweet-talkin' a little ol' yeller gal. Got him a scrubbin' and some new togs, too. You seen anything of Awsheel?"

"I'm told Monsieur Galante is in Paris." Taggert frowned thoughtfully. Haldane wandered to the doorway and glanced down to the courtyard in time to see a gigantic Negro in mud-splashed trousers and bare to the waist, disappear into the servants' quarters. He had been hatless, his pants wet to the knees as though he'd been swamp wading. Taggert turned at Haldane's exclamation. "Nothing much, Judd. I just saw a big midnight-black Negro . . ." He added details. Instantly they remembered the wide-brimmed straw hat they'd spied in the barouche that morning. Speculation was immediately banished, however, by the arrival of Lustrous in fresh cotton garments, bearing a cross-wick lamp, and followed by three other servants carrying food. Lustrous remained to serve a dinner of crisp salad, roasted fowl, brandied peaches and red wine, followed by thick black coffee.

Lustrous, folded napkin over one arm, ventured a question. "Majuh, suh, y'all rec'lek de stohy in de Good Book 'bout de Sama'itan whut failed heself among thieves? We done ouah good Sama'itan deed wid dat bay-rooche t'day, but ouah stohey tu'n out de opposite. Dese folks ain't no thieves."

"What are they?" Taggert asked. "You pick up any ideas?"

Lustrous sobered. "No, suh, Ah does'n'. Some, queah bunch of niggehs, calls deyself West Indians. Talks de French talk. When Ah inqui'es 'bout de madame, dey shuts up an' meks lak dey don't unner'stan' whut I says. Whut y'all meks of it?"

"First," Haldane observed, "it's discourteous to show curiosity about our hostess. Secondly, the Negroes are probably from the West Indies, Santo Domingo, say . . . I'll have more coffee, Lustrous."

Dishes were finally removed and Lustrous

departed. Taggert sighed contentedly. "Garth, we sure traveled a far spell from yesterday's war. Regardless what you say about Lustrous's curiosity, I'm doing some wondering. I thought things were tough for the N'Orleans folks under the Feds. But I asks you—what's all this? Good food, liquor, cigars—loads of servants. Could be the madame ain't a Southern sympathizer, even if she tooken us in. What you think?" Cigar smoke drifted lazily in the room as Haldane stated he hadn't yet formed an opinion. He yawned wearily, settled back in his chair, and advanced an idea the lady might be a neutral.

Taggert jeered. "Hah! Ain't nobody could ever convince me she's a neuter. Might be the madame is workin' secret with Yanks, just pretending to be for the Confederacy. Hell, you and me might find ourselfs in a blue-belly hoosegow tomorrow. Maybe she's feathering her own nest and workin' with the Fed Provost-Marshal. All this liquor and food. The South ain't had the like in years. The more I think on it, the more I'm ready to get our hawsses and—"

He paused, swearing disgustedly. Haldane, eyes tightly closed, was sound asleep in his chair. Taggert glared at him a moment, then relaxed. He rose, turned the lamp low and tiptoed off in the direction of his own room. Ten minutes later he too was fast asleep.

It was nearing midnight when Haldane roused.

He yawned, stretched and walked to the gallery beyond the doorway. A soft breeze carried the marshy odor of Lake Pontchartrain. Below the gallery, moonlight silvered the oleander leaves and pink camellias. A fragrance of honeysuckle reached his nostrils. No one was in sight on the gallery or the courtyard below, though a far corner at the front of the house was lighted brightly and a confusion of many voices could be heard. He returned to his room for a cigar then descended to a seat on a stone bench flanked by a tubbed banana tree and a huge terra-cotta jar placed to catch rainwater from the slanting roof.

He lifted his gaze to the brightly lighted corner room on the second floor. Draperies at open windows moved with the breeze. Must be some sort of gala affair transpiring; a reception of sorts, perhaps? Still, there was no music, only a steady drone of voices. Once a drape moved widely and Haldane caught a glimpse of a number of dark-clothed men. Clinking sounds reached his ears. A servant emerged from the rear of the house, bearing a tray with an array of glasses and bottles. The man moved silently across the courtyard, mounted to the balcony by a corner stairway and vanished into the lighted room. A moment later the door reopened and two men emerged, accompanied by another servant.

Haldane tensed: the two men now descending to the courtyard wore the uniforms of Union soldiers. Haldane drew deeper into the shadows. A long pent-up breath escaped him when the pair turned toward the tunneled passageway leading to Dauphine Street. He saw the heavy oak doors swing open, then reclose. From beyond came the sounds of horses' hoofs on cobbles. The servant returned to the upper room.

An hour Haldane watched, the cigar dead between his fingers. There were similar departures of at least fifteen blue-clad officers, by twos and threes, one either injured or so drunk it was necessary he be carried, unconscious, by servants. Any air of gaiety on the part of the departing officers was lacking; rather their conversation seemed to be tinged with grumbling, or a kind of hopeless anger. This, more than anything, persuaded Haldane to postpone awaking Taggert to relate what he'd witnessed. Finally, with a shrug, Haldane ascended to his bed. It was past three in the morning before all lights in the Maison Galante were extinguished.

CHAPTER 6

Morning light was streaming through the jalousies when Haldane awoke. Lustrous, in neat cottonade, was already moving about the room, arranging shaving tackle. Haldane asked about Taggert. "Yas-suh," Lustrous chuckled, "Mistah Judd he jist layin' dar, blowin' off he sleep lak a chuffin' steam-injine. Me, suh? Ah does mahself ve'y finely, in-deed. Sech rations Ah done consume." Later, when he had served a breakfast of ham, small sausages, biscuits and honey, followed by coffee, the Negro announced he wished to share his winnings.

"Share your winnings? What winnings, Lustrous?"

Lustrous delved into a pocket and tumbled on the table a diverse mass of currency. There were several U.S. silver dollars, two small gold-pieces, three worn Spanish coins, French francs, two U.S. bills, a sheaf of Jeff Davis shin-plasters and a quantity of paper money from the presses of the State of Louisiana and the City of New Orleans, not to mention a number of cheaply printed shin-plasters issued by various city merchants, plus two outdated lottery tickets. Haldane stared in amazement. "Great Scott! Where did this come from?"

"Dese West Indian niggehs 'nitiated me inter a game whut's played wid two li'l blocks of ivory wid black spots. You th'ows 'em on de flooah and when de rat spots come, y'all wins—"

"Don't act so damn' innocent." Haldane laughed. "Rolling dice isn't new to you."

"Dem West Indians don't know dat, suh," Lustrous replied smugly.

Haldane refused a share of the spoils and Lustrous departed. The morning drifted past. Robert, the major-domo of Maison Galante, brought in the latest newspapers with word that his mistress would be pleased to receive Major Haldane at five that afternoon. A yellow girl, head bound in a blue madras *tignon*, arrived to "make up" the room. Later, alone, Haldane examined the newspapers, *New Orleans Picayune* and *L'Abeille*, the latter in French. The news in the *Picayune* was depressing with its talk of Reconstruction for the South, votes for Negroes, and the proposed confiscation of Confederate property. A department to be known as the Freedmen's Bureau was causing considerable debate among politicians in Washington. Pennsylvania's vindictive old Thaddeus Stevens was still preaching his hymn of hate against the South. Haldane laughed over an item proposing to give forty acres and a mule to each former slave, wondering if Southern planters owned sufficient to effectuate such a plan. There seemed to be little news concerning Texas. Haldane put aside the papers and glanced through slim copies of *De Bow's Review* and *Harper's Weekly.*

Taggert entered while he was examining the magazine and Haldane told his sergeant of the Union soldiers he'd seen departing the previous night. "By Gawd, Garth, I don't like the looks of it. The madam has some tie-in with Yank bastuds. Have you talked to her yet?" Haldane stated that he was to "be received" at five that afternoon.

Taggert grunted. "Received, huh? Like there'd never been a war, and she ain't goin' to let nothing interfere with her society lallygaggin'. But, could be, she ain't owin' us nothing at that. I been fed good." Taggert finally announced he reckoned he'd go back to his room and catch up on some sleep, and he didn't think he'd ever get caught up on his drinking.

At five o'clock Haldane presented himself at a door only a few steps from his own around the wrought-iron balustraded balcony, and was ushered into a large room furnished with con- siderable taste, at the front of the house. Haldane judged from sounds beyond a double doorway to an inner room, that Mme. Galante would appear presently. Robert withdrew and Haldane seated himself on a Louis Seize sofa of ivory white, upholstered in dark velvet. A table stood at one side, arranged with silver, linen and a spray of jasmine in a crystal holder. Air stirred gently the cream damask drapes at the opened fanlights of long windows. A pair of Ciceri gouaches in gold frames graced an ivory wall; Aubusson carpeting covered the floor. Over the fireplace the marble mantel held a pair of Chinese lion dogs, exquisitely carved from rose quartz, guarding between them stalks of copper-hued iris in a *famille noire* vase of the K'ang Hsi period.

Haldane caught Mme. Galante's terse voice from an inner room, "*C'en est assez*, Babet," and a moment later a handsome little mulatto maid appeared, offering Haldane a flirty eye as she passed through the room. Mme. Galante entered an instant later, glowing in white Indian muslin, lined with green silk, cut low at the shoulder line. Her rounded arms showed through transparent sleeves, tied at wrists with narrow black moire ribbon; a brooch of carved aventurine at her breast, and a ring, comprised her only jewelry. There was a single creamy camellia in the burnished chestnut hair, and she brought with her a faint fragrance of vetiver.

"Have you found yourself comfortable, M'sieu?" she asked, the words throaty, liquid, as Haldane rose. Never more so, he assured her. She said abruptly, "Babet states that you are 'andsome. Scarcely could I restrain her from peeping in. Of a verity!" And at his question, she explained, "Babet. My maid. She is a baggage that one, and made of a complete raving. '*Quel homme*! *Quel le taille*!' What a man! Of a masculinity—*zut*! Girls are all of a madness these days."

Laughing softly, Haldane asked if it were permitted to ask her opinion. Mme. Galante shrugged shapely shoulders. "Of men? I will tell you, M'sieu, the Major, in a man I seek something more than appearance. Masculinity, *oui*. Of good features, of a certainty. But, I ask myself, what is behind the eyes? Is the mind and the courage sufficient—?"

A servant with a tray holding bottles and tobacco interrupted, and withdrew after pouring two drinks in small glasses; Haldane refused tobacco and sipped the icy-cold drink. The taste was new to him and he expressed appreciation. Mme. Galante explained it was from the formula of a local apothecary, a recipe brought from San Domingo, a matter of cognac and bitters poured into an egg-shaped cup and some secret ingredient added. It was called a *coquetier*. ". . . and look you, M'sieu, when I was in New York"—her laughter brought music to the room—"I introduced it to friends. They made a misinterpretation of the name and termed it a cocktail. And served in the glasses small feathers from the tail of a rooster."

He joined in the laughter, meanwhile wondering when she had been in New York. And why? She made no explanation. When he endeavored to thank her for her kindness to him and his men. Mme. Galante brushed aside his thanks and lighted a small thin cigar of pale tan. Blue smoke drifted through the room. She explained that she had invited him late in the afternoon that they might dine together, and to also allow time for her beauty *siesta.* That, Haldane assured her, was something he was amazed to learn she ever required, and discovered, at once, there were small dimples at either side of her red mouth.

"Now I am certain, M'sieu, that you are of the true South. Those of the North never make so graceful the comment." She asked questions and Haldane spoke a little of his hopes to rebuild White Hawk Acres, of the affair in North Carolina and the long ride that followed. "I have heard of these guerillas," she said. "And this man of the black mask, you never learned his identity?"

"He had left before I recovered consciousness. A girl, Laure Gabriel, to whom I'm greatly indebted nursed me back to health. Judd Taggert managed miracles . . ."

Robert arrived to serve food brought by two servants. Haldane and Mme. Galante moved to the table, seated opposite each other. Candles in seven-branched candelabrum cast glimmering reflections on the silver. There were various dishes—rice, a bisque of shellfish, a light heady wine, roast duck, gumbo and sweet biscuits. Followed a different wine and the inevitable black coffee. Robert withdrew leaving the man and woman in a circle of candlelight which scarcely reached the far corners of the room. An unlighted gas chandelier was suspended overhead, but it remained unlighted to Haldane's satisfaction.

Conversation languished momentarily. She glanced up and caught his gaze resting on her left hand. He explained he was admiring her ring. "I've never seen one quite like it before."

Slipping the ring from her finger, she passed it across, telling him it was of a kind of jade known as "mutton-fat" jade and very rare. It was cut from a single piece of stone and of a creamy tallow color streaked with crimson blotches. On the face of the stone was carved a circle bisected with certain lines, which she explained was called a *chou*, a symbol of longevity, or good fortune. "The peach and bat," she explained the rest of the carving, "signifies happiness, long life, wealth"—she shrugged—"like most Chinese symbols."

"I've never seen a stone quite like it," Haldane commented, "but I suppose there are others. Or am I wrong?"

"If so, I do not know of its existence. The ring belonged to *mon pere*—my father—though his finger was too large for the wearing. Before the war he collected many Chinese objects, but now, *helas*! most have vanished. A few only remain—

Sacrebleu! You have no interest in such past things. I but waste your time."

This he denied, but she failed to continue. Abruptly, her infectious laughter filled the room and she banged a spoon in her hand. "This way we get nowhere, you and I, M'sieu, the Major. We are like strangers, *n'est-ce pas*? Not so? You speak but little, but all the time I can see the revolving of wheels in your head. *Tiens!* Of what do you think? Of my jade with crimson markings? You are telling yourself, perhaps, that it is most appropriate? That *I* am the jade—the crimson jade?"

He assured her that wasn't so. She smiled rather wistfully. "Then you are more generous than most. But do not deny that you think of me? Who I am? Where is my husband, the M'sieu Achille Galante? Why we possess so much of fine food in a time of war that even now, for the South, is not ended? I am a problem, is it not? When you consider the Union *soldats* you witnessed departing last night? You puzzle what it is they do here?"

Haldane's face crimsoned and he apologized for eavesdropping. She denied he'd eavesdropped. "You were enjoying the peace of my courtyard. A servant saw you. You puzzle about those Union *soldats*. You knew I did not speak truth when I said Boaz took me for an airing yesterday. This much I read in your eyes. *Zut!* I think I will tell you something of me, Angelique Galante."

She poured fresh coffee for Haldane. A dish of jumbal biscuits, whose rosewater and almond flavor intrigued Haldane's taste, was placed closer to hand. Cigars, cigarettes, were nearby. Angelique Galante lighted another of her pale, slim cigars, smoke spiraling delicately from her thin nostrils.

"First, I shall speak of Achille Galante. It is true as Robert has told you, Achille is in Paris. It was a marriage arranged by my father. Achille and I we mean exactly nothing to each other. That Achille"—scornfully—"he has the spine of an oyster. Lacking of the shell! Of a verity! The war he feared greatly, so it was arranged for him to depart. Since then, there have been many Achille Galantes." Her dimples deepened. "Not at all in the way you think, M'sieu." Embarrassed, Garth Haldane tried to tell her he had no thoughts whatever in the matter. "*Fi donc*! It is of no consequence. I am aware of men's thoughts. I am no child. Look you, how many years do you think I have?"

Instinctively, feeling he should put the figure higher, Haldane guessed her to be twenty-one or -two, and saw her white teeth flash ironically. "Now I am certain you are of the very deep South. It is two years since I have seen eight-and-twenty—so much I shall admit. And you are a great fool if you believe me. No, no, enough of such gallantry. It is of my various husbands I would speak—those men who have found it necessary to remain for a time in New Orleans before making an escape from the Yankee swine. It is on the records I have a husband, one Achille Galante, a citizen of France. If the use of that name has protected me and aided certain fugitives, where is the harm?"

Abruptly, it dawned on Haldane she had been, to state it bluntly, an agent working in the Confederate cause. She continued: numerous men had lived at Maison Galante under the name of Achille Galante. A great deal of information had filtered through Angelique's slim fingers from time to time, and reached Southern leaders.

She talked on. Certain vague remarks gave Haldane the impression she had received aid from the British Consul in New Orleans. When he expressed surprise, she admitted nothing but merely shrugged cryptically her white shoulders, pointing out that everyone knew Britain to be the South's great friend. England had hoped for a Confederate victory. Undoubtedly true, Haldane conceded. Still, he didn't quite comprehend whence came all the food, nor how so many servants were maintained. Surely, the Federals must grow suspicious. Had she claimed French citizenship? Angelique's dark eyes sparkled.

"That I would not do. I am a *citoyen* of the South." She continued: dishonest men can always put aside suspicions, so long as their palms are well greased, and in the Army of Occupation there were many dishonest men. As to methods—perhaps it would be well to go back a few years. She was, Angelique told Haldane, the daughter of a French father and French-Spanish mother, the latter long since dead. The father, Arnaud Galante, had maintained for many years, a fashionable *maison de jeu*, a gambling house, in New Orleans, operated the past ten years with the assistance of his daughter.

"Two weeks," Angelique Galante explained, "from the time the Union General Butler entered New Orleans, my father wished me to have the protection afforded by a married name. He sought out the spineless Achille Lavache, a penniless native of France, who wished frantically to return to Paris. Money was paid, papers drawn before a notary. I became the wife of Achille Lavache, with the arrangement that I retain the name, Galante, with my father, in the business of gaming. The French consul arranged matters. Achille departed. One week later *mon pere* was executed for refusing to salute the flag of the United States—shot to death in the Place d'Armes by a drunken Yank soldier."

"He did nothing but fail to salute?" Haldane was unbelieving.

"That was all. My father was loyal to the South. So he was shot. M'sieu, the Major, you could not believe the things that occurred in New Orleans under the rule of Beast Butler, who arrived in '62. Under Butler, monstrous doings prevailed. Should a young, unmarried girl show the least contempt for a Union officer, she was arrested as a prostitute." Her lips tightened. "Do you wonder so many girls failed to show their contempt and instead—*Mon Dieu*! I grow bitter again. It is sufficient to say that under this vile General Butler such suffering came to New Orleans that both French and British Governments made formal protests to the United States. But until General Banks succeeded Butler, this city was a veritable hell for Southern sympathizers."

She smiled suddenly and poured wine. "But not for me, Angelique Galante. At least I have lived well. For a time I was desolate. And then I considered. If you cannot defeat openly an enemy, it is best to pretend to join him. So I took the Oath of Allegiance."

"To the United States?" Haldane sounded disappointed.

Her white shoulders lifted in a gesture of contempt. "What would you? The oath, what is it? So many empty words. *Zut*! Could I have helped the Confederacy by refusing the oath and leaving to starve the servants? When one could accomplish good in other ways? Of a verity, no!"

Haldane conceded that, as a woman, she might be right. Mme. Galante continued, "There is this

Colonel Albro Isham, on the staff of the Federal authorities here, who is never averse to putting into his pocket extra gold. Colonel Isham—there is a specimen!—controls in many ways much influence. I request of him an audience. When we meet, I mention our well-known Maison Galante and remind that Union officers must have recreation. At once he perceives and, for a percentage of gains, I receive from Colonel Isham permission to reopen our gaming establishment.

"And so"—a contemptuous snapping of fingers—"at once I am successful. There are many of the military here, also Northern speculators and government politicians. The business of gaming is *tres* excellent. With United States gold one can purchase such food as required from a certain scoundrel in the Quartermaster's Department, who imports only the best for the so-called higher-ups. That also was arranged by Colonel Isham."

"Meanwhile," Haldane said disdainfully, "this Isham grows rich preying on his own kind, knowing they have small chance of winning at your gaming tables—or am I wrong?"

"What think you?" Her magnificent eyes sparkled with delight. "Should one suffer compunctions taking from an enemy?" She added details: the men who operated her game were Southern sympathizers; other Confederates wearing blue uniforms took part in her games of chance. Chance? All was fair in love and war, especially war. And the South did not recognize defeat, nor deny the struggle still to come. The battle to save the South from extinction, Mme. Galante declared, was just beginning, though few realized it. "We fight for our very lives. In Washington exist monsters who will be content only when every Confederate is dead and his property confiscated." Haldane commented that "monsters" was a rather strong word. She said hotly, "What otherwise call those devils who have cast Jefferson Davis in a dungeon, with shackles of iron about his ankles and friends not permitted to see him?"

"President Davis?" Haldane exclaimed incredibly. "In irons?"

"Of a verity! You will see. So do not judge too harshly, Major Haldane, if those who play in my gaming saloon do not always win. I fight this war in my way. And there are times when they do not lose. One must offer encouragement until they return for a final plucking. Some complain, but such complaints never go beyond Colonel Isham. It is an arrangement of perfection. The Maison Galante gains money with no interference. Once each month, the pig-dog, Colonel Isham, calls to collect his percentage of winnings. Yes, pig-dog! He is a dog with the small eyes of a pig in a swollen carcass."

A ghost of a shadow crossed her features.

"Of late, he has become of the most pressing. He wishes more than his percentage. He sends flowers and bonbons. I give them to Babet to put with the trash. Consider, M'sieu, a pig in love. It is of the most disgusting. Filthy animal!"

Before Haldane could comment the angry color left her cheeks. "And now, Major Haldane, you are aware of what I am and what I do."

Haldane thanked her for her confidence. She shrugged. "*Diable*! It is nothing. In a day or two you will depart. Perhaps I can help others after you. But, my word on it, this war is not over. I believe worse is yet to come, if the North gets it way. The fight—" A small clock in a case of gold and crystal chimed the hour. "*Hein*!" she laughed. "This time, how it makes passage. M'sieu Haldane, it arrives the hour for one to change. One's guests of the evening will be arriving."

Haldane was instantly on his feet, making the proper remarks. Angelique interrupted, a small, thoughtful frown gathering below the fringed chestnut bangs. "It occurs, M'sieu, you may care to visit this evening our gaming saloon. I am certain it is of an extreme dullness in your room. Perhaps, if you had the inclination—?"

Haldane mentioned his clothing; they were scarcely fitting for such an occasion; he couldn't appear in his gray uniform which, anyway had been taken for cleaning. Mme. Galante offered to furnish a blue uniform. Haldane frowned; that would be very distasteful. She assured him he had no cause to worry; proper clothing could be provided.

A mischievous light entered her eyes. "I don't think you would care to pose as Achille Galante, recently arrived from Paris—no, you have not enough of French—a moment! *Regardez-y bien!* I have it. You shall be Mr. Garth Haldane, a British subject, recently arrived from Jamaica to consider investments here, now that there exists so much unrest among the blacks in Jamaica. Or it could be salt is your interest—rock salt recently discovered on Petit Anse Island. It has drawn many speculators. Which is it, M'sieu, sugar or salt?"

"Sugar, by all means," he laughed. "But could I pass as a Britisher? I don't believe I talk like one."

She rested one white hand briefly on his arm. "Pouf! You think those stupid Yankees will note a difference, when your accent is already different from their tones of a harshness?" Haldane reminded her all Yanks weren't stupid. Scornful laughter denied this. "Yankees who come night after night to Maison Galante to be rooked, can be nothing less than stupid. So, it is settled. This evening when you come I shall already have spread a rumor regarding the Englishman who arrives here. My guests will be most intent on the business that brings them here. No great attention will be paid to one tall Englishman who comes here to pursue an inquiry regarding sugar. In my house, M'sieu, the Major, you are completely safe."

CHAPTER 7

Haldane returned to his room to find Taggert awaiting him at a table loaded with dishes and the remains of food. "Didn't know if you'd be back or not, so I told them to bring the vittles here," he explained. "I sure et elegant." Haldane explained he had dined.

Lustrous came, removed the dishes and departed. Taggert lighted a cigar, asked, "How did the madam receive you?" Haldane commented wryly that the question lacked a certain delicacy. "Judd, understand please, this isn't a fancy house."

Taggert snorted. "Then what's all this tie-in with the Yanks? Ain't no gen-u-wine Southern lady livin' like we see it here, less'n there's somethin' off-color going on. All right, all right"—at Haldane's pained protest—"I won't say another word, only maybe you can tell me exactly what kind of house is it?"

"First, Judd, you're completely wrong. Let me explain exactly what Mme. Galante is doing . . ." From that point on, Taggert listened with relatively few interruptions to an account of the information Haldane had received that afternoon. When he had concluded, a look of amazement had formed on Taggert's saturnine features.

"By Gawd, when I'm wrong, ain't nobody else can be wronger," he admitted. "I should've knowed better, after I pumped Lustrous. He insisted the place was all hunky-dory. So the madam is really on our side, after makin' a deal with this crooked Colonel Isham. Did she mention our pullin' that barouche outten the swamp, say where she'd been?"

"The subject came up. No explanation was made. By the way, that ring you saw is of jade. Madame Galante claims she's never seen another like it. You're sure it was the same as the masked man wore?"

"Well, natural, I ain't certain—" He broke off as Robert knocked and entered, a suit of gray clothing and the accessories folded over one arm, explaining they were for the major's evening wear. Now, if M'sieu would be pleased to try on these things . . .

There were a ruffled white cambric shirt and black stock, moonstone studs and cufflinks. The trousers were rather small at the ankles, as were the sleeves at the wrists of the long high-waisted coat. Civilian clothing felt strange after four years of gray uniforms. Haldane studied the effect in the pier glass, while Taggert sat, slack jawed, in amazement. Robert's white teeth gleamed. "Though not quite of de latest fashion, M'sieu Haldane," the old Negro pronounced. "I think dese things do you very properly. If dere is nothing else . . . ?" He bowed and withdrew.

The instant the door closed, Taggert demanded explosively, "Now what in hell goes on?" Haldane informed him he was, for the present, Mr. Garth Haldane, British subject from Jamaica. In Louisiana for the sole purpose of studying sugar investments. Taggert swore. "The whole business sounds *loco*!" he stated bluntly. Haldane explained he was to visit the Galante gaming *salon* that evening. "Damned if I like it, Garth," Taggert scowled. "Too risky. Remember you ain't ever surrendered. You get messin' among blue-bellies, no sayin' what might happen."

Haldane interrupted. "Terry's Rangers have run bluffs before. I'm not worried. Remember, Mme. Galante knows we're eager to return to Texas. She's had considerable experience passing men through the city and across the river. When the time is ripe for us, she'll let us know. As her guests we owe a respect to her wishes. I was invited to attend tonight. It may prove amusing. Who knows what information I may pick up. If she is right, and I think she is, a war for the South's very survival is just beginning." Taggert subsided reluctantly, but continued grumbling, finally departing sulkily for his room.

At ten that evening, Haldane arrived in the gaming salon, a spacious room with three glittering chandeliers of crystal globes, within which burned lambent gas flames, suspended from the ceiling. The furniture was of San Domingo mahogany, upholstered in deep red. On the plastered walls, tinted ivory, were paintings in gold frames—a landscape signed Corot, a small oil still life by Boudin, a draped nude of Ingre's, a portrait of Baudelaire by Courbet, among others, reflecting the taste of the late Arnaud Galante. Beige drapes were at the windows; the polished parquetry floor was bare of carpeting. The salon possessed a weary air of lingering elegance not entirely dispelled by the various gambling tables. In one corner poker hands were dealt; there were two roulette wheels sunk in green-covered tables; there were baccarat and *chemin-de-fer*; it was inevitable that a pair of lay-outs should be devoted to faro, a game that first reached the U.S. by way of New Orleans.

Mme. Galante's croupiers, their faces stony, impassive, were clothed in neat black. A continuous babel of conversation from blue-clad officers, formed an undertone against the rattle of poker chips and the measured voices of croupiers. Cigar smoke drifted in thin layers. A servant passed, bearing drinks. Near the doorway at a small desk, a thin girl with mask-like features the exact shade of a withered gardenia exchanged with various players, from time to time, colored chips for bills and coins.

Haldane looked about for Angelique Galante and found her seated on a sofa against one wall, languorously plying a black-edged ivory fan. She had changed to a gown of some gossamery material displaying to advantage the alabaster whiteness of arms and shoulders. Her dimples showed momentarily as she motioned him to a seat at her side. Three Union officers had just departed, bowing. Two more instantly arrived to present compliments. Angelique presented Mr. Garth Haldane, recently of Jamaica. Drinks of combined mint and bourbon arrived. Remembering a few contacts with Englishmen, Haldane managed to keep his speech short, clipped; he spoke no more than necessary and assumed a slightly bored air. The precaution was scarcely necessary: the officers paid him but slight attention. It became increasingly evident to Haldane, now, that gaming wasn't the sole attraction of Maison Galante. The officers gathered about Angelique murmured awkward compliments; many of them were quite young, callow.

Leaving Angelique talking animatedly to an admiring circle, Haldane proceeded to the gaming tables. A Union infantry officer who had once visited Jamaica endeavored to involve Haldane in conversation about the country. Affecting a rather supercilious air, Haldane informed the man that Jamaica, now that the Negroes were kicking up so much bally rot and ruining sugar production, was "beastly, y'know, too unutterably beastly even to warrant chit-chat," and moved quickly away to pause at a table of *chemin-de-fer* players, standing well back to watch the manipulation of the cards. After a time it occurred to Haldane that the banker had retained the deal for an unusual number of coups. All seven players were in uniform, but as the banker continued steadily to win, Haldane suspected he was no military man, but rather one of Angelique's Confederates, as was, Haldane felt quite certain, a second blue-clad player seated across from the banker.

Haldane eyed the sharpers with considerable distaste, even as the thought came to him that these Northerners being rooked were of the same forces intent on crushing the South completely. In the final analysis, was this cheating at cards any worse, say, than luring an enemy into ambush, as Terry's Rangers had so often done? He drew a deep breath and moved to the nearer of two roulette tables where he stood watching the play, until his attention was diverted to the farther of the roulette lay-outs, by angry words from a tall, bulky-shouldered man in the uniform of a U.S. Cavalry captain. His face was flushed with drink. His heavy black mustache was curled at the ends; his eyes were a very pale blue.

A young lieutenant with crisp blond hair was trying to quiet the captain. "Oh, come now, Captain Gratton, sir, you can't expect to win every time." The words ended in a tittering laugh.

"But, blast the luck, Purdy," Captain Gratton

fumed, "I don't seem able to win at any time. I don't trust these damned—"

Hastily, Lieutenant Purdy interposed certain words and indicated the table where the croupier was already preparing the next spin of the wheel. "*Messieurs, faites vos jeux!*" Players began to place their bets, the angry Captain Gratton among them. Haldane frowned; the man's features with their heavy black mustache, thick brows, blue eyes, gave the impression he'd met the man somewhere. But where? The voice of the croupier intruded on Haldane's abstractions, this time in English. "Make your bets, gentlemen. Last chance."

The wheel was already involving the small ivory ball running madly across the frets. Impulsively, Haldane drew from his pocket the eight-sided gold-piece entrusted through Lustrous by Laure Gabriel, so long ago, and tossed it at random upon the green, marked cloth, giving no heed on which number it had fallen. "*Rien ne va plus!*" came the voice of the croupier. "The betting is closed, messieurs." The wheel was already slowing down. Anxious comments were heard about the table.

The croupier lifted his rake. Haldane's attention was already drawn back to Captain Gratton who, immediately upon the cessation of the wheel where he'd been betting, broke into angry cursing. Other men drew away from him, while

Lieutenant Purdy resumed placating words. "I'm stating here and now," Gratton spoke in a loud rasp, "that this game is crooked. I demand—"

"M'sieu!" The cold, fish eyes of the croupier rested bleakly on Captain Gratton, the tones were chill. "You will please to name the exact sum you have lost at this wheel?" Taken aback by the frigid voice, Gratton ceased his cursing. The croupier repeated his query. Sulkily, Gratton named an amount. The croupier eyed him steadily a moment and Gratton mentioned a figure less than that first given. From the pile of coins and gaming chips before him, the croupier deftly sorted a few gold-pieces and silver coins which he shoved disdainfully across the table. "There is your money, Captain Gratton. You will please to not return to Maison Galante again. We have only disinterest in patronage such as yours." The croupier's gaze shifted quickly about the table. "Gentlemen, the play resumes. *Faites vos jeux!*"

Face crimson, the scowling Captain Gratton scooped up the money and barged angrily away from the table, shoving roughly past other players who cast irritated glances after him, before turning back to the wheel. Haldane followed Gratton with his eyes, saw the enraged captain striding toward Angelique Galante. Instinctively, Haldane started to follow, when the voice of the croupier nearest, arrested the movement. "A moment, M'sieu Haldane. You forget your winnings," the man politely pointed out. "Or did you wish to play them?"

Amazed, Haldane found himself a winner of a sum in excess of four hundred dollars, which he crammed hurriedly into his pocket, thinking, *Now I can repay Laure Gabriel her loan,* without stopping to consider if he'd ever again see her. His good fortune momentarily ignored, he turned once more, gaze seeking the bulky form of Captain Gratton.

Gratton had found Angelique Galante by this time. His face was contorted angrily, his tones harsh. Haldane, approaching, caught the heated tones, ". . . you can't act this way. I refuse to leave."

"Refuse?" Angelique's dark eyes snapped. "Captain Gratton, I speak for your own good. It would be inadvisible for you to remain. My croupiers are entirely trustworthy. I prefer to take the word of the man who returned your money."

Lieutenant Purdy, behind Gratton, tried to get in a meek word. No one paid him heed. "Damn it," Gratton insisted, "that wheel is crooked. I know! I've got a new system. I simply can't lose on a game run honestly."

A thin smile touched Angelique's lips. "The more reason you are not welcome here, Captain. Let us say, we are afraid of systems—" Noting Haldane's approach, she turned away. "Ah,

M'sieu Haldane, you enjoy yourself one hopes."

"Until quite recently," Haldane replied. "Can I be of service?"

Her eyes warned him off, but before she could reply Gratton was facing her again. "I tell you, Madame, I refuse to be kicked out in such fashion—"

"*Que diable!*" Angelique turned furious. "Refuse? I have only to call and you will be thrown out. Is it that you wish? Now, please—"

"You're going to hear me out," Gratton insisted stubbornly. "Three nights in a row I've played here and—"

"That is, possibly," Haldane interrupted with a certain insolence, "three nights too many. Madame Galante has made it plain you are unwelcome. That should conclude the matter."

Gratton turned his suffused face to Haldane. Lieutenant Purdy squealed nervously, "It's the Britisher, Haldane, Captain Gratton."

Gratton growled, "You'd better keep out of this, Haldane. You English have interfered enough in the war. Take my advice. Keep away from here. The games are all crooked."

"That has yet to be proved," Haldane stated coldly. "At any rate, this is no place to discuss the matter. If you care to step outside, I'll listen to any proof you have to offer . . ." Without waiting for Gratton's reply, Haldane crossed to the doorway and stepped to the balcony, standing deep in shadow. Below, the courtyard was flooded with moonlight.

A moment later, Gratton emerged, followed by Purdy. A colored servant hurried after them with their hats. The door closed. Furiously, Gratton confronted Haldane. "Now, you listen to me, Mr. Britisher! You've interfered in what is none of your business, just as your damn government interfered to help the Confederacy. The South got what it deserved and England will, too, if it doesn't stop meddling. The whole situation is crooked, crooked as the games that Galante woman is running—"

At that point, Haldane knocked him down. Purdy bleated a shrill protest, rushed at Haldane and received a back-handed slap that sent him sprawling over a tubbed oleander standing against the wall. Gratton came slowly to his feet. Haldane struck him again and the captain went hurtling toward the stairway, tripped on the first step and went rolling to the bottom, where he lay for an instant stunned. Purdy regained his feet, dodged around Haldane and rushed down to the courtyard. Gratton, shaken by the fall, was rising clumsily to his feet. He stood glaring up at Haldane, mouthing curses. Crimson flowed from his nose and, lifting his arm, he drew the cloth across his face, smearing the blood over his chin. He coughed and started to speak. Purdy caught at his arm.

Haldane stared down at Gratton, eyes widening, something abruptly dovetailing in his memory. Urged on by Purdy, Gratton was walking unsteadily toward the tunneled entrance. Haldane started to descend to the moonlighted courtyard, but reached the bottom stair only in time to hear the big entrance door close and the clatter of hoofs in Dauphine Street.

Haldane turned toward the gallery again, face thoughtful, blowing softly on his bruised knuckles, and then paused to see Angelique descending. Reaching the bottom, she demanded to know what had happened. "Nothing to speak of," Haldane replied. The Negro servant returning from the entrance was detained while Angelique questioned him in rapid French. At his reply, she whirled back to Haldane, eyes sparkling excitedly. "You struck the swine!"

Haldane answered that he seemed to remember hitting both of them, adding that, for a moment, he had lost his temper. Regrettably, he added, "I just couldn't help myself. The instant I saw Gratton I disliked him. Intensely. I—I think I've seen him before. In a way, I suspect he had a legitimate grievance when he said your wheel was crooked."

"Not that particular wheel," Angelique replied promptly. "Not tonight. That wheel was of the utmost integrity. *Tiens*! You think it would be wise the house wins all the time? Even with an honest wheel the percentage remains with the house. Gamblers must win on occasion, else they do not return to Maison Galante." Haldane remembered now to mention the money he had won at roulette. A shrugging of slim shoulders. "It was your luck. Another time you may lose if you have not the intelligence to remain away from my games."

Neither made a move to return to the gambling salon. Moonlight cast a silver mantel over the courtyard, placing bronze highlights in Angelique's burnished hair. Honeysuckle cloyed the air with a sweet fragrance. Haldane guided Angelique to a stone seat. "I must," she told him, "return to the gaming room," though she made no effort to rise. A servant bringing ice to the second floor passed. Angelique spoke to him. Within minutes he returned bringing a cigar for Haldane and one of her slim cylinders of pale tobacco. Haldane held a match and watched the smoke form gray arabesques as it drifted from her thin nostrils. There was a rich mellowness to his own cigar. His thoughts returned to Gratton; he hoped no trouble would arise from the quarrel.

"Nothing I cannot prevent," Angelique assured him. "A word to Colonel Albro Isham and we shall—how do you say it?—cook of the Gratton's fish of a complete thoroughness." Mostly they sat in silence, Haldane ever conscious of the presence of the slim woman at his side and the fragrance of vetiver hovering about her. Occasionally something was said that brought sweet laughter to her red lips. Time drifted on languid wings until there came a sudden pounding at the entrance.

A servant came hurrying to answer, returning an instant later with the blond Lieutenant Purdy, distinctly nervous; it was apparent he had been drinking. Angelique started to speak, but Haldane rose. "You'd best let me handle this." Then to Purdy, "Now what's up?"

Purdy drew himself to rigid attention, though swaying a trifle. "Lieutenant Purdy, at your service. I have the pleasure to represent Captain Kayser Gratton who demands satisfaction of Mr. Haldane—"

"Satisfaction?" Haldane demanded. "What the devil does he mean? I knocked him down twice. What more does he want?"

Purdy gulped. "You don't seem to understand. You insulted the captain. He has consented—er—he demands, well—if you'll name someone to represent you—"

Angelique, at his shoulder, exclaimed angrily. "They are a pack of imbeciles. It is a duel Gratton asks. Because there was much of dueling here in Louisiana, these idiots of the North find it entertaining to keep alive the custom. Someone has persuaded Gratton—"

"That's it, a duel," Purdy stated, hiccoughing a

little. "Either Mr. Haldane apologizes, or Captain Gratton demands a meeting on the field of honor—"

"Field of honor!" Haldane exploded. "This is ridiculous. Does he insist on being knocked down a third time. You've both been drinking too much. Get back to your quarters and sleep it off—"

"I advise you—hic!—to apologize, Mr. Haldane. Captain Gratton is an expert with a pistol—"

"How does he know I'll choose pistols?" Haldane demanded. "As the challenged party I have the choice of weapons. I may decide on mud-bricks at fifty paces. Or bare fists. There's been enough killing the past four years—" He broke off. "No, by Jupiter! I owe him something, if he's fool enough to want it—"

"Captain Gratton—hic!—intends to teach you Britishers a lesson. He instructed me to tell you to bring a six-shooter—"

"I'll try to scrape one up."

"M'sieu Haldane," Angelique put in, "leave to me these matters. I can stop all this—"

"I'm not sure I want it stopped." Haldane's anger was rising. "Gratton is the one who needs a lesson. I'll give him satisfaction."

"Y-Yes, sir," Purdy stammered. "If you'll name your representative we can discuss conditions—"

"I will represent M'sieu Haldane," Angelique

stated curtly, her anger also rising. To Haldane, "Such imbeciles! They know nothing of the code of duelling. I advise, M'sieu Purdy, you consult one who comprehends such, that you and Captain Gratton may not make even greater fools of yourselves. M'sieu Haldane, the weapon you wish?"

"Six-shooters, as Gratton requests—at ten paces."

Purdy made choking sounds. "Ten paces? Ten paces!" He protested it was incredible. "Haldane, a man couldn't miss at that distance."

"You grasp the idea," Haldane said grimly. "I do not intend to miss. The place is up to you. Let's make it"—glancing at the moon—"six hours from now. Or dawn. Where?"

Purdy swallowed hard. "There's a spot not too far from here—"

"I know where these duels are held," Angelique interrupted. "We shall be there. Now, please to leave at once, M'sieu, the Lieutenant."

When the sounds of Purdy's horse had died away, Angelique said, "This insane business I do not like. A word to Colonel Isham and—"

"I don't believe you care to be under obligation to this Isham." Besides, he added, he didn't want the duel cancelled. "Gratton invited trouble. The Yanks have become insufferable. Through Gratton I can teach the Yanks a lesson, perhaps."

He escorted Angelique back to the *salon*, while

113

she instructed him in certain duelling procedure. "Eat nothing before this meeting. Perhaps, a little coffee, or cognac for the nerves." She added she would see that horses were ready in time. Haldane thanked her and strode around the balcony to Taggert's room, where he found the sergeant sleeping. Taggert yawned and asked thickly if anything unusual had happened.

"Judd, I won four hundred dollars at roulette." That, Taggert grunted, was prime news. "Also, I'm fighting a duel at sunrise, Judd."

The bed creaked suddenly. "Gawdamighty! I knowed nothing good could come of you goin' to that gamblin' saloon. Some Yank bastud, I suppose." Haldane said he had guessed correctly.

CHAPTER 8

The moon was down and it was pitch-dark in the courtyard when Haldane completed writing certain letters: to a banker in San Antonio, and one or two friends and relations. He considered a few words to Laure Gabriel, but wasn't certain if she still remained at the Boar & Tankard. Instructions to the banker mentioned the girl and obligations due her; similar instructions included Judd Taggert. Lustrous hadn't been forgotten. Taggert entered the room, clothed in a long coat that had been brought him. He commented that the gambling "saloon" was dark but a light shone from the madame's quarters. Haldane indicated the letters on the table, near the lamp. "You'll see these are mailed, Judd, if anything happens."

Taggert blustered, "Ain't no Yank bastud can kill you—"

A knock at the door precluded Robert's entrance with word that Madame Galante was waiting. He brought over one arm a long coat and broad-brimmed felt hat. Haldane asked a question and learned that Lustrous was sleeping, and knew nothing of the duel. When Robert had left, Taggert asked jealously, "What's she going for? We don't need a woman in a business like this."

Haldane replied that until this minute he wasn't

aware Mme. Galante intended to accompany them. "I don't like it," Taggert growled. "I know we should have kept straight through to Texas. Damn it, Garth, you don't act like you took this business serious." Haldane indicated coffee, cups, that had been brought some time before. Taggert refused with an oath.

Haldane said imperturbably, "I've reached the point, perhaps, where I see small sense in placing too much importance on anything, Judd. We had four years of taking things seriously, and what did it bring us. Make no mistake, I shall do my best to kill him. Generally speaking, I consider that the practice of duelling indicates a lack of intelligence on the part of the participants, but in this case it is my intention that Gratton shall die. I'll tell you why—later." Haldane got his gun and other equipment, donned the hat and long coat.

Taggert suggested a drink of cognac for his nerves. Haldane laughed. "For the dampness perhaps, not my nerves." A quill pen stood in a miniature celadon bowl, held in place by a quantity of shot. Haldane plucked out one of the pellets, tossed it in the air and caught it on the back of his extended hand. The pellet moved slightly, then there was no movement at all. "Nerves?" Haldane tossed the pellet in the bowl.

"You'll do, Garth. I should have knowed."

They extinguished the flame in the lamp and descended to the courtyard. A lantern held by a servant cast a small circle of light. Horses stood near. Haldane caught Angelique's low greeting. "There was no need for you to come—" he commenced.

"*Au contraire*," she replied. "It is because of me you are involved. Look you, I can still prevent this insane duelling—" Haldane interposed to point out quietly they'd discussed that before, that he didn't want the duel stopped. She could see, couldn't she, that interference could only result in branding him a coward.

"*Quel homme*," Angelique sighed, "so like a man to think of his pride rather than his life. *Helas*! Let us start then." She moved into the circle of light. Startled exclamations were voiced by Haldane and Taggert.

It was a transposed Angelique Galante; she was dressed as a man, the shining chestnut hair tucked beneath the wide-brimmed black felt hat that came low on her forehead. The black trousers were tucked into boots and a long black cloak hung from her shoulders. Haldane said quietly, "Only the mask is missing—and the derringers." And to Taggert, "You were right about the jade ring, Judd."

Taggert rose gallantly to the occasion. "Leastwise, Garth, we got the chance now to thank madame for saving our skins—"

"*Zut*! It was nothing. And you recognized my ring, M'sieu Taggert? I grow careless. That day you extricated my barouche I recognized you both. Instantly. But come, I shall explain while we ride."

They mounted and moved out to the street. A servant followed on a fourth horse. The animals' hoofs made ringing sounds on the wet cobbles. Haldane felt mist on his face. There wasn't a star to be seen. The horses turned on Ursuline Street. Angelique rode between the two men, the animals moving at little more than a walk. An almost imperceptible graying now appeared along the eastern horizon.

"And so now you know," Angelique was saying, "that the operation of Maison Galante has not been my sole activity." Haldane asked questions and she furnished details, mentioning secret work for the South, travels through Northern states and the South, gathering information.

Taggert blurted, "Then you were a spy for our side—?"

"Say, instead, I was used to gather and transport information gathered by intelligent spies. As a woman I traveled where men could not. On forged papers I traveled everywhere, by train, horseback. At times I was a lone widow, returning to relatives in the North. *La*! What an hypocrisy! Or I had leave to visit a husband prisoner in the North, or a brother. I transported funds to certain men—copperheads, traitors to the U.S., who objected to Lincoln. Sometimes I carried gems to

118

be exchanged for gold in New York or Chicago. That gold bought men who would obstruct the North. Do you remember the draft riots in New York when the mobs went wild, burning, killing, destroying the draft office? The police were powerless. It gave Washington such a fright that for a time drafting of men ceased."

The horses' hoofs clopped steadily on. Angelique said, "There was an arrangement to release eight thousand Confederate prisoners at Fort Davis. Once free, they would have seized Chicago, controlled banks, telegraph wires, railroads. Then more prisoners could be released in Illinois and Indiana. *Helas*! That plan failed. But with most plans success was achieved."

Haldane mentioned the Boar & Tankard. Angelique explained, "Throughout the South were established frequent points of contact where I had friends. The Boar and Tankard was one. I had left a train and taken to horseback. I arrived by the rear, and hearing voices I saw what was taking place, the guerilla swine! *Zut*! It was nothing. A mask, derringers, and the entrance dramatic."

"Anyway, it turned the trick," Haldane said, and asked concerning Laure Gabriel. "I could never figure her out. Our questions concerning you were met with blank stares or word that she knew nothing."

Angelique laughed. "Ah, a smart one, that

Laure, and not so stupid as she led you to believe. One of our best operatives for that sort of job. An agent of the most dependable, Laure Gabriel." She interrupted the men's amazed remarks. "Almost in speaking of the past, we forget what lies ahead."

They'd stopped before a low brick house with a lamp burning in one window. A short dumpy man in frock coat and a weathered silk hat emerged, carrying a small black satchel. Angelique introduced him as Doctor Alceste Desparvieu, explaining that the doctor had been in attendance, during his life, at many *affairs d'honneurs*, and was fully conversant with the duelling code. The doctor shook hands. He was around seventy, Haldane guessed, as he mounted the horse brought by the servant, leaving the servant to return home on foot. They continued, turning left on Esplanade Street. Haldane and Taggert dropped behind, while Angelique and Desparvieu carried on a desultory conversation in French.

The darkness was lessening. There were fewer houses to be seen. A dank breath from swamps assailed their nostrils. It became light enough to see an occasional moss-hung oak. A half hour later they crossed a stout bridge of cypress logs built across an estuary, and almost immediately found themselves entering a grove of superb live-oaks whose ancient gnarled limbs were festooned with long strands of Spanish moss. Angelique signaled for the horses to stop.

They dismounted in wet grass beneath one of the oaks whose leaves dripped a continual moisture. It was considerably lighter now, though the enveloping mist appeared impenetrable, intensifying the surrounding silence and enhancing the slightest sound with an unusual clarity. A flock of wild duck winged far overhead. Dr. Desparvieu held a lighted match for one of Angelique's slim tan cigars. She watched Haldane intently. "M'sieu Haldane," she finally queried, "you have no nerves?" Haldane confessed quietly that as yet he felt no trepidation; that, perhaps, would come later. She spoke rapid French to Desparvieu. The doctor turned his lined face toward Haldane, shrugged, muttered something that had to do with "*sans peur*," in a level tone.

The mist thinned; trees lost their ghostly aspect and emerged in clearer perspective. Haldane glimpsed a faint salmon coloring seeping into the gray eastern sky. The sun should rise shortly, dissipating the mist that enveloped Louisiana earth.

Taggert said suddenly, "Somebody coming." The clumping of hoofs and rolling wheels sounded across the bridge of cypress logs. An open carriage with driver and one occupant took form in the grayness. Behind were two riders, Gratton and Purdy.

Angelique said despondently, "I hoped the fools would not appear." She spoke rapid French to Desparvieu and slipped behind the horses, with a few additional words to Haldane. Haldane gathered that the doctor was to act as his second, and he warned Taggert, regardless what happened, to keep his head.

Desparvieu had stepped forward to greet the stopped carriage, while Gratton and Purdy continued on a short distance. A man was alighting from the carriage, almost a replica of Desparvieu in looks and dress. The two advanced, doffing shabby silk hats and shook hands; their French was unintelligible to Haldane and he turned to Angelique for explanation.

It appeared, she told him, that Gratton had been advised to have with him someone conversant with the duelling code. They had found in the Street of the Fencing Masters—Conti Street—Mons. Narcisse Bossuet, one as well versed in duelling matters as Desparvieu. The two were known to each other. Gratton and Purdy were now dismounted. Purdy hurried to join the two Frenchmen. Taggert also approached them, and, more leisurely, Haldane. The men were introduced. Taggert glared at the Yank but said nothing, to Haldane's relief. The two Frenchmen took control of matters. Purdy asked nervously, "Mr. Haldane, you still insist on firing at ten paces?"

Haldane made it clear he was adamant on that point. The Frenchmen stared at him, unbelievingly, but agreed that, as the challenged party, he was within his rights. Gratton's blustering tones intruded, "What's the delay, Purdy? I came out here to kill a limey meddler." He came striding toward them, not noticing Angelique shielded behind the horses. He added harshly, "Haldane, I'm surprised you had the nerve to show up. Got a gun, I suppose."

Haldane eyed him steadily a moment, then nodded toward his gun in Taggert's hand. Taggert's face burned crimson; with an effort he remained silent.

The two Frenchmen, Purdy and Taggert continued their discussion. Impatiently, Gratton swung away from the group and lighted a black cigar. Bossuet eyed him with distaste, as though regretting he had allowed himself to be drawn into the affair. Haldane felt anger building within himself. Angelique, behind the horses, was largely hidden from view. Probably the smart thing to do; should it become known she had become involved in a duel concerning a Federal officer, it could make trouble. Haldane didn't blame her for remaining apart.

Taggert spoke to Haldane, a few steps off. "We've agreed Doctor Desparvieu will officiate. He will say, 'Ready, gentlemen,' then count, 'One, two, three. Fire.' You're to be in shirtsleeves." Haldane removed his long coat, the one beneath it, also his hat, and strode over to place the doffed garments on the saddle of a horse. Gratton had been complying with similar instructions. Taggert spoke again, " 'Nother question's come up. Is more'n one shot to be fired by participants, or do you quit after one shot? As the challenged party—"

"One shot," Haldane stated clearly, "will be all I'll require."

Purdy gasped. Gratton's jaw dropped. He started a protest then thought better of it. "Me, too," he said lamely.

The cap-and-ball revolvers were being loaded by Purdy and Taggert. There was little to choose between the two Colt's .44 six-shooters, both showing considerable past wear. The two Frenchmen studied the sky, considered the evenness of the earth, or lack of same. They finally agreed on a stretch of turf a few yards off. Side by side, they took several steps, then stopped. With his heel, Desparvieu drew a line in the damp earth. Again, in unison, they paced off ten wide paces. Bossuet drew a line across wet grass. The "field of honor" had been laid out; it ran roughly north and south.

Taggert and Purdy hurried toward their principals, Taggert saying, "Garth, the doc tossed a coin for position. I called 'heads.' You won. I picked that far end, though there's not much difference. But if the sun should break through it won't hit you in the eye. You'd best take your place now and get settled. I think the background will be okay. With this misty atmosphere . . ."

Haldane started toward the opposite end of the "field of honor," as Gratton took a position at the nearer end. Gratton's voice, as the two came within speaking distance, was a snarl, "Haldane, I should have killed you last night. There'd been no need of a second meeting." He looked furious.

Haldane paused in mid-stride, facing Gratton. "Second meeting?" he said almost pleasantly, voice not carrying to the others. "You're mistaken, Gratton. It's the third, at least. Have you forgotten the Boar and Tankard Inn, near Bentonville? I doubt you're a captain in the U.S. army. They don't offer commissions to guerillas." Bowing curtly, he passed on.

Gratton had gone red, then white, eyes staring, mouth agape. He tried to speak but words wouldn't come. As Haldane passed the horses Angelique confronted him, the black silk handkerchief tied across her lower face, only her superb eyes showing beneath the hat brim. He caught the intent, if not the exact words, and the ". . . my heart goes with you, M'sieu Haldane." That, he replied, was even more good fortune than he had dared hope for. Behind them, he caught the startled exclamation from Gratton.

He swung around. Gratton's staring eyes

seemed bulging from his suffused face. He gazed at Angelique as though hypnotized, open mouth giving him a rather imbecilic expression. Angelique turned, long black cloak swirling about her booted legs, and went back to the horses.

"Purdy," Gratton bellowed, "who—who's that feller in black—?" His voice failed him.

Purdy shook his head, calling back, "Take your place, Captain Gratton." He was already moving away from the others.

Haldane took up his position, glancing down at the heel-mark drawn in the dark earth. Taggert hurried up and gave him the cocked gun. "Primed and ready, Garth. You're to hold your gun at your side and not raise it until Doc Parvieu counts 'three' and says 'fire.' Is that clear? Purdy loaded all chambers in Gratton's gun. I loaded five for you, as usual. Only one shot's to be fired, but you never know what that Yank bastud might have in mind—"

"Not so loud, Judd."

"Don't fret, Garth. I know I got to keep calm-like." At that moment Desparvieu called to him, and Taggert moved away. Desparvieu stood equidistant between the duellists, Bossuet at his side. Flanking them were Purdy and Taggert, faces anxious. Gratton, gun in hand, was toeing his mark, but kept turning his head toward the spot where Angelique waited. Haldane surveyed the positions, the cocked gun in his right hand, held at his side. Tiny beads of moisture formed on the tawny hairs of head and mustache. A slight breeze stirred the mist to swirling activity. He was aware that his white shirt would show up strong against the dark tree at his background. Beyond Gratton, was gray mist, moving, undulating. It might make shooting difficult. . . .

Desparvieu's icy tones cut in, "Gentlemen, the signal is about to be spoken." He waited a moment more. Haldane and Gratton faced each other, turned slightly sidewise. Haldane waited, gun held at side. The damp air biting through his shirt carried a certain chill, but he was unaware of it in the icy rage that now possessed him. Desparvieu continued, "Gentlemen, award me your attention, please. Ready! One!" A pause. "Two!" A second pause. "Three—fire!"

Gratton's arm swept up surprisingly fast, but Haldane's gun was even quicker. He didn't take time to bring the weapon to arm's length, but fired the instant he could bring the muzzle to bear on Gratton's body. Gratton's shot was almost an echo of his own, the man's leaden ball flicking the shirt over Haldane's ribs.

Through the lifting haze of black powdersmoke, Haldane saw Gratton whirled half around by the heavy impact of the .44 bullet. The man strove to right himself, as the cap-and-ball slipped from his weakening grasp; then he pitched awkwardly to earth, an ominous dark stain appearing on his shirt front. Haldane stood as before, gun muzzle still extended, feeling the glacial anger slowly drain from his mind, as he gazed on the still figure huddled on the earth. He saw Taggert hurrying toward him, heard the relief in Taggert's voice. "You were good enough, Garth, but he was faster'n I figured."

"I was good enough," Haldane said quietly. He saw Desparvieu, black bag open, crouched over Gratton's body. Purdy and Bossuet stood near. Angelique remained near the horses.

Purdy approached, voice cracking a little. "The doctor says Captain Gratton is dead."

"I intended to kill him," Haldane said coldly. "He brought it on himself, not only last night, but long ago."

"I don't understand," Purdy said uncertainly. "You said something to him, and then he saw that man in black. He was unsettled. This business must be investigated—"

"It will be far better if it isn't," Haldane informed him. "I've an idea his military papers are forgeries. During the war, Gratton headed a gang of raiding guerillas." Purdy said he found that hard to believe, but was shaken when Haldane told him he could bring proof, if necessary. That, apparently, was to end the matter, particularly when Haldane mentioned that the U.S. army frowned on duelling.

The sun had started to break through as Haldane, Angelique and Taggert were recrossing the bridge over the estuary. Desparvieu had remained behind with Bossuet and Purdy. Angelique had removed her mask, but kept her hat brim pulled low. ". . . but, cripes, Garth, I don't see how you recognized the bas—the guerilla scoundrel—"

"Nor I," Angelique put in.

"Back there at the Boar and Tankard, I had a few minutes of clarity. I remembered a man blackly bewhiskered. Last night, when I hit him, he bled freely. Lifting his sleeve to wipe off the blood, he managed to smear the lower part of his face. In the half light of the courtyard, the darkened chin gave an impression of whiskers. Abruptly, it occurred to me who Gratton was. I feel he got no less than he deserved."

CHAPTER 9

It was decided, Angelique Galante concurring, it would be best if Haldane did not again visit the gaming salon. Another incident, similar to the Gratton affair might lead to more serious consequences, involving not only Haldane, and the discovery of his presence at Maison Galante, but bringing about the disruption of a certain plan forming in Angelique's very attractive head. A week after the duel there'd been no outcry over Gratton's death. How Purdy covered things up, they never learned, at least so far as Angelique could learn. Her plan was broached two days later, when she sent word there was a matter of importance she wished to discuss with Major Haldane when he had leisure.

Taggert was present when Robert brought the message. "Leisure," the sergeant snorted. "As if you had anything else, or me, neither. I'm aimin' to stir some dust toward Texas—"

"I'm as eager to get started as you, Judd. That may be what Mme. Galante wants to talk about. We've already accepted her hospitality too long."

An hour later, he presented himself at Mme. Galante's door and was shown in by the flirty-eyed Babet, who instantly withdrew. Angelique, in severe thin black with a narrow collar of lace and long sleeves, raised one white hand to motion him beside her on the Louis Seize sofa, and indicated whisky and tobacco on a small table before them. "My father," she stated abruptly, "was a man of much wisdom."

That, Garth Haldane replied, could be but half the story; undoubtedly a beautiful mother had contributed the other half . . . "M'sieu Haldane," Angelique interrupted, "I did not ask you here for the purpose of accepting compliments, graceful as they may be. There is a time for such speeches. That time is not at present." Subdued, Haldane agreed. He saw now she was all business; there was none of the provocative seductiveness of which he'd been intensely aware on previous occasions.

"You are not listening, M'sieu. What I wish to say may be of the utmost importance to you, if you have any use for money." Haldane begged her pardon and answered that he had always found the possession of money convenient. She continued, "I present certain facts"—enumerating them on the fingers of one white hand—"One: you have said that you require the means to rebuild your White Hawk, in Texas. Two: you are a man of courage—no, no! That was proved in your meeting with the Gratton guerilla. I have use for a man of courage, M'sieu Haldane. Three: as I remarked previously, *mon pere* was a man of much wisdom. Four: at the present time, because of a scarcity, cotton is worth one dollar the pound."

Amazed, Haldane remarked that at that price a bale of cotton would bring close to five hundred United States dollars. In England, about a hundred pounds. It was unbelievable!

"*Hein*! You have much to learn then, M'sieu. Something over a year ago, the Confederate General, Kirby Smith, burned one-hundred-fifty thousand bales, that the cotton might be prevented from falling into the hands of the Yankee General Banks. I remember well a newspaper deploring the close to sixty million dollars that ascended in flames, while mills in England were shut down and workers starving." She continued: England must have cotton. The manufacturers in northeastern United States demanded cotton, with little to be had. Cotton speculators, even before the close of the war, had been ranging through the southern states, with and without Federal sanction.

Haldane agreed that all she maintained could be true, but what had he and this feverish demand for cotton in common?

"You shall see, M'sieu Haldane." She said again, "*Mon pere* was a man of much wisdom. He foresaw what war would bring. There were many who said New Orleans would never be captured. He knew the contrary. New Orleans held out—let me think—one year and a little more. Then arrived the capture of our city and the hell-work of Beast Butler—but I do not like to remember that. When Admiral Farragut began the bombardment of the city, my father realized the end drew near. He did not wait until the U.S. fleet sailed up the Mississippi, breaking the great chain across the river, as if it were composed of thread. What think you he did?"

Haldane waited, eyes questioning. Angelique Galante continued at once: "Here and there were cotton warehouses not yet broken into. The owners were frantic for fear of a loss. My father went, *tout de suite*, with hired wagons. As much cotton as possible he purchased and secreted in this house, so the Yankees would not find it. He paid only one or two cents a pound for cotton that is now worth one dollar. *Nom d'un chien*! You should have been here to witness. In every room, except the gaming *salon*, bales of cotton. Scarcely was room left to make breathe, or move around." Her sudden laughter like silver bells afloat on a rippling stream filled the air, as she reached for one of her slim cigars. Haldane held a flame for her. Blue smoke sculptured delicate arabesques through the room.

"Then, when my father was killed, I experienced a fear. The United States had declared cotton contraband, and in this house were more than one-hundred-fifty bales. M'sieu, the Major, I was frantic. Of a verity! Then, I gave thought to how *mon pere* would face such a situation. I made plans. When the Yankee soldiers arrive to make an inspection of all houses, I place on the front of Maison Galante, a sign which read, 'Yellow Fever.' Because of New Orleans' many epidemics, it was a notice to cause trepidation, and the *soldats* filed quickly past."

She drew on the pale tan cigar and placed it on a crystal tray. "Next, I have to think of transporting the bales to a place of safety, where they will not be discovered by Yankee swine. It is now less than one year since the last bale was removed from this house. I worked at night, with the help of servants. I trust them to the utmost. Emancipation, what is it? *Pouf*! My Negroes are not interested. They know I will take care of them. Even now, should anything happen to me, all I have will be distributed among them. I have made a testament to such effect. *Aussi*, that was as my father intended."

A secret hiding place for one-hundred-fifty bales of cotton, Haldane supposed, would be difficult to locate. "M'sieu Haldane, not so difficult as you think. That, my father had also planned for, and, at the time of his death, he had already under construction, a small warehouse for cotton. I saw to the completing of that building, and maintain there, much of the time, three Negroes, though often one of them, Big Indigo—"

She interrupted herself. "You have noticed

here, perhaps, a very huge Negro?" Haldane replied that he had seen in the courtyard such a man, the day Mme. Galante's barouche had been rescued from the swamp. Hatless and bare to the waist. He had been mud-splashed; his trousers soaked. . . .

"That is Big Indigo," Angelique cut in. "He is of the most faithful and understands completely the storing of cotton and its care. Of all men, he alone can find his way, unaided, to the hiding place of my cotton bales. I know something of the way, but not so well as Big Indigo. Wait! I shall show you."

She procured from a rosewood cabinet a map showing southern Louisiana and a portion of the Gulf of Mexico, and returned to the sofa, where the map was spread across their knees. "You note here where the Gulf touches land? Here is Breton Sound and Chandeleur Sound, southeast of Lake Borgne. Now over here"—indicating with a tracing finger—"you see a great many islands, near the mainland, as though *le bon Dieu* had sprinkled them about like holy water. Many are low, covered only with marsh grass. Others bear trees. Now, right here, you will see, is located a sandy spit, jutting from the mainland a short way. Around the edge of this spit is a growth of trees, and among the trees stands my cotton warehouse."

Haldane appeared a trifle skeptical. "That may

provide a hiding place for cotton, but why is it so difficult to locate?"

"First, the building is hidden by the height of the trees. Second, from the mainland, at a distance, it is not seen because of intervening swamps and cypress growth. Third, from the Gulf it can not, this place, be distinguished from numerous other islands also possessing a certain timber growth, and the waters are too shallow to allow passage of anything except a small vessel, among these many islands.

"Of course, M'sieu Haldane, my place could be discovered in time, but the Yankees are stupid, and the fishermen and trappers of the swamps are loyal to the South. I planned to hold my cotton until peace really came, but now I no longer dare. Also, at one dollar the pound, now is the time to sell. You have heard, M'sieu, of the order of the United States Government to confiscate all cotton controlled by the Confederacy? No? It is so. Already Treasury agents swarm like hornets through the South, seizing all cotton they find."

She poured bourbon for Haldane and a small glass of wine for herself, with scarcely a break in her speech. "Especially *now.* I have told you of this Colonel Albro Isham who grants me protection, for a price, to operate my gaming *salon.* Colonel Isham is of the most greediness. Somehow he has learned—it was common knowledge at the time of the buying—that my father had bought these bales of cotton and hidden them away. Now, Colonel Isham grows ambitious and thinks to find that cotton."

She smiled. "The day you rescued me from the swamp, Colonel Isham's men had been following. I had thought to throw them off, by traveling in the carriage, as if for a drive of pleasure. But we took saddled horses, as well, at some distance, to negotiate where the barouche can not travel. It was planned I would change later to man's clothing from a small valise I carried. When the men of Colonel Isham could not be thrown off, we postponed the trip, and to lead them astray turned north. Big Indigo with the saddle horses, cut off through the swamps, and led Isham's men deep into the swamp until they became lost. If they found their way back, I never knew." Disdainfully, she shrugged.

"By then, I, too, had become uncertain of the way. Boaz, my coachman, knew nothing of the way. We made what we considered a short cut, with solid footing for horses and barouche, across a swamp. All advanced well until we had nearly reached the shell road, then we became—how do you say it?—bogged down? Until you arrived with Sergeant Taggert. Much later, Big Indigo returned home. You see, only Big Indigo and I know the way through the swamps to the cotton-house, and I am not always too certain without him. Others may lose the way and become devoured by alligators."

Not a cheerful prospect, Haldane conceded; he thought of water moccasins and other hazards.

Angelique continued, "Now there is this Mr. Rupert Downson, an Englishman, who is interested in my cotton. M'sieu Downson, when the Yankees first attacked New Orleans, also took advantage of the people's panic. He purchased for almost nothing a sailing vessel which the owner was prepared to burn, rather than see it fall into the hands of the hated Yankees. It is not a large vessel; it had been built for pleasure—a yacht, it could be called. M'sieu Downson puts it to a practical use. He has connections in Jamaica. He sails there, occasionally, bringing back certain goods of advantage to the Confederacy, though the so-stupid Yankees imagine he voyages only for pleasure, back and forth in the Gulf. They fail to comprehend he travels so far. As a British subject, he enjoys a certain immunity from U.S. prying. Also, he brings in diamonds which may be purchased more cheaply in British lands than here. Many Yankee officers wish to buy diamonds for their women in the North. If they have not paid a United States duty, what difference? So, M'sieu Downson sails often to Jamaica and back—"

"Good Lord! Jamaica must be a thousand miles from here—"

"At least so much," Angelique Galante agreed, "but what is distance when profits are excellent? *Parbleu*! M'sieu Downson is of a type most adventurous. Now, then. I have made a contract with M'sieu Downson. He has a willingness to carry my cotton to Jamaica. From there it can be shipped to England, which has a great need to keep its mills running. The money received, excluding expenses, can be divided in three portions—to you, to M'sieu Downson, and to me. Does this interest you, M'sieu the Major?"

Haldane, puzzled, failed to comprehend why he should be included in such plans. "M'sieu Downson insists on dealing through a white man. It is a prejudice insane, but what would you? Because of Colonel Isham's spies, it is not practical that I journey to the cotton-house, lest he learn the hiding place of the bales. I am in need of one with white skin to help me. Colonel Isham has no knowledge of your presence here. There is little you would have to do—see that bales were placed on a barge and receive money from M'sieu Downson which you would bring to me. That is all—nearly. There exists always the danger of an encounter with Colonel Isham's spies, if by accident they discovered your trail. Comes then the danger of shooting, capture, or death. It is a situation to be considered. You could include in your plans, M'sieu, the Sergeant Taggart."

Haldane frowned thoughtfully, while Angelique Galante moistened her red lips with wine, then continued, "If you agree to this, there will have to be a meeting with M'sieu Rupert Downson. It is best he does not visit here. I can not risk going to him, or sending you direct to him from here. But if you met by arranged accident to discuss the matter . . . ? All he wishes is to be assured of your identity. He cannot risk an involvement between his government and that of the U.S."

Haldane hesitated and reminded her of his desire to reach Texas. How long would such a transaction require for fulfillment? "This sailing vessel of M'sieu Downson's is, as I said, of small size. He could ship on one trip fifteen bales. At most he should be done in a year—ten months—perhaps, with good fortune, less."

Haldane ran fingers thoughtfully through his tawny hair, scratched his chin. "Lord, I'd hoped to be in Texas within the coming month."

Angelique Galante nodded calmly. "That may be accomplished, if you insist. But consider, M'sieu. To be of a complete success in Texas, you require money. Affairs in Texas are not good at present for soldiers of the Confederacy. In business they do not have it easy. By working with M'sieu Downson and me, you will be enabled to gain sufficient cash to rebuild your White Hawk Acres. *Tiens*! Even if ten months are required, how else can you gain an approximate twenty thousands of dollars in so short a time. That amount I guarantee you. And, M'sieu Haldane, has your visit at Maison Galante proved so uncomfortable that you dread so small a time as ten months more here?"

A white hand moved to rest lightly, appealingly, on one of his own; the dark eyes raised to his. He stammered something regarding his extreme present comfort at Maison Galante. "But—but I know Judd Taggert," he said, "will kick up all hell when he hears this. I owe much to Judd. He must be considered—"

"So? Let him kick up the hell," Angelique replied quietly, "and when he has subsided, point out the advantages of what I propose. He is a man of intelligence. I think he will listen to reason when he sees that we are beating the Yankee thieves. Explain clearly to him the war still continues." That, Haldane assured her, as he rose to leave, was exactly what he intended doing.

CHAPTER 10

Taggert did "kick up all hell," as Haldane had predicted, but eventually quieted under Haldane's determined stand. Finally, throwing up his hands and stating in no uncertain terms that he didn't like the idea, a-tall, Taggert conceded he knew of no better method of returning to Texas with twenty thousand dollars in pocket and at the same time giving the Yanks another "whuppin'." Haldane sent word to Mme. Galante before Judd had an opportunity to change his mind. She held a brief meeting with Haldane and gave him certain, precise instructions.

Two days later, instead of leaving by the front entrance of Maison Galante, where some chance spy of Colonel Isham's might see him, Haldane crossed the courtyard and passed through the kitchen to the rear of the building where a tall oleander lifted crimson blossoms against a high wall, completely concealing the small door built into the plastered bricks. He emerged through this doorway into a second courtyard, where an old Frenchman, seated in a chair, gave him a pleasant "*Bon jour*," as though this an everyday occurrence. An exit to the next thoroughfare lay beyond, and presently Haldane was heading south along the Bourbon Street *banquette*, in search of a certain address where he was destined to meet and recognize Rupert Downson by a prearranged set of phrases. Haldane had been told that the address was that of a cafe of sorts, where the patrons passed the time in playing chess, such times as they weren't drinking. Perhaps they did both.

There were relatively few blue-clad soldiers to be seen on the streets. They were, it was understood, being discharged rapidly, or being sent to Texas where the threat of the Emperor Maximilian's activities were potent. The military in New Orleans were fast being replaced by a horde of Northern opportunists and speculators who had arrived carrying carpetbags—empty carpetbags, if rumors were to be believed. The Northerners pouring in came with only one dollar and the shirt on their backs—and never changed either, it was said.

Haldane passed but few people. The day was clouded; a heavy mist permeated the atmosphere, dripping from overhanging balconies to the *banquettes* below, and seeping gently into Haldane's seersucker suit and broad hat of finely woven straw. A blue-uniformed officer approached along the *banquette*, and Haldane felt himself perfectly secure; in one pocket now reposed papers attesting him to be Garth Haldane, a British citizen of Jamaica, with temporary residence out Tchoupitoulas Road—at least far enough to make an investigation improbable. Taggert had been furnished similar forged papers, by Angelique Galante, though to date he had sulked at Maison Galante, refusing to leave the house.

The address Haldane sought proved to be an ancient corner building with wide double-doored entrances, topped with fan-shaped windows, opening on two streets. A wrought-iron railing ran around the second-story balcony. Haldane strolled casually through an entrance and found himself in a large room of cool, shadowed recesses, with heavy arches across the high ceiling, supported by round columns of plastered brick. A staircase ascended from the rear to a narrow balcony with a wooden railing. A few men at the marble bar were occupied with tall glasses containing a milky-green fluid. Players at chess and domino tables made the requisite moves and, with little or no comment, continued to study the pieces before them. A small unoccupied table, bearing a chessboard and pieces, caught Haldane's eye and he waited there for his man and certain signs by which he was to recognize him. A pleasant air of serenity hovered over the place; the chair at the table was comfortable. Attendants apparently didn't bother with patrons unless service was demanded.

The individual who abruptly materialized across the table from Haldane lacked the appearance of a British seafaring man. He was slight of form with dark, fine skin and hair; his black eyes seemed abnormally bright. Haldane hadn't seen him enter, nor was this the approach he was prepared for. The dark man wore the clothing of a gentleman and was hatless. Making a deep bow from the waist, he seated himself at the table, across from Haldane. No word had been spoken.

Speculation ran rife through Haldane's mind: could this slim, graceful man be one of Colonel Isham's spies? He appeared to be around thirty. Rupert Downson was to have spoken certain phrases. There was a distinct charm in the dark man's smile; in his bright eyes, though, there existed a vague quality giving an impression of a mind living in the past rather than the present. He spoke finally, tones low, cultured, musical. "If you'll be so kind as to accept the white pieces," he murmured, generously offering Haldane the first move.

It might be best, Haldane concluded quickly, to accept matters as they came, until something definite could be determined. They commenced setting out the board. Haldane was only a fair chess player, the type that studies well each move before touching a piece. His opponent, on the other hand, acted with swift decision, one shapely hand, graceful as a woman's, darting to the board the instant Haldane made a move. He was unpredictable, his tactics dazzling. He sacrificed a queen, a rook, momentarily raising

Haldane's hopes of winning, until—"Check and mate, sir."

Haldane realized he had lost the game in something less than twelve moves. His opponent continued, "It is plain you are not in practice. Shall we have another?"

Before Haldane could reply, they were interrupted by the arrival of a worried-looking man, wearing the striped apron of a servant. "M'sieu Paul," he said in relieved tones, "at last I find you. We have searched everywhere. You should not expose yourself in the damp weather. Your health—" He paused, directed himself to Haldane. "Your pardon, M'sieu. He has an illness."

Haldane's opponent had gained his feet. Again he made his courtly bow. "Another time, sir, I trust . . ." And then he was being led away by the servant who had thrust a hat on his dark head, the incident passing so quickly that others in the cafe had scarcely taken notice.

Haldane was still staring at the doorway through which they'd vanished, when a voice across the table asked, "I say, would you be interested in a game?" The accent was definitely British.

This, Haldane realized, was better, the exact words he had been expecting to hear. He gave the correct reply, "I have only a little time."

"I've been known to make my moves quite quickly," the other repeated the words of the ritual. He dropped into the chair opposite Haldane, a tall, angular man with broad shoulders, somewhere past thirty-five. His chiseled features were set in a weathered face, and his blue eyes had the far look of the sea in them. "Name's Downson, Rupert Downson." He removed the broad-brimmed woven straw hat, ran bony fingers swiftly through his thatch of sandy hair, the hand pausing to drop thoughtfully, tugging, at the lobe of one ear. "Owner, y'know, sailing vessel, *Perdita*."

The movements, the words, were the correct ones. "I'm Garth Haldane, a British citizen from Jamaica." He picked up a white and black pawn in either fist and extended them. "Choose, please."

"I prefer the white always," Downson laughed shortly and touched one of Haldane's hands. Haldane extended the black pawn. They began setting the pieces on the board. Some of the stiff formality left Downson's manner. "Silly rigamarole, what, Haldane? But have to make proper certain, y'understand. Isham's men damnably busy these days. Ambitious beggars. With General Banks conniving with all these Northern blighters—well—can't be too careful."

He motioned to a passing attendant. A tray was brought, holding a tall green bottle, sugar, glasses of chilled water. Downson dipped sugar with perforated silver spoons and rested them across the edge of the glasses. A greenish-yellow liquor was dripped through the sugar, forming opalescent arabesques as it mingled with the chilled water. Downson's long tanned fingers moved deftly through the process, then passed one glass to Haldane. "Try that. Guaranteed to make the darkest day bright."

Haldane had been talking of the dark-complexioned man with whom he'd played chess. Now he paused to sip the drink and acknowledge its merits. "For a time," Haldane said, "I thought something had gone amiss with our plans. However, whoever he was, he could play chess. It was amazing. I felt helpless against him."

Downson put down his glass, nodded. "No doubt, Haldane. I arrived as he was being taken off. Congratulate you!"

Haldane failed to comprehend. Downson explained, "One day you'll boast to your grand-children that you lost a game to Paul Morphy, the one and only Paul Morphy. Greatest chess master the world has ever seen. Or will ever see."

Haldane acknowledged the name was vaguely familiar. "Vaguely?" Downson snorted. "Never admit that to a real chess player. Morphy was a genius. Only thirteen when he defeated the great Lowenthal. I saw him in Paris, in '58, whip six of the best French players—with a blindfold across his eyes. Moves were called out to him. Without seeing the boards, he kept six games going in his head. This is a day for you to remember. He doesn't, I'm told, play any more. Too much play when young, I've heard. Mind affected. Quite! That sort of thing. Don't understand his getting here. Likely out for a stroll. Wandered in. Saw the board—well, old habits, y'know. Any real chess players in here, they'd had him on their shoulders in a trice. Definitely. Oh, quite! I'm talking too much. Effect wormwood has on me. Another?"

Haldane declined a second drink. He wanted to talk about cotton. "Nothing much to talk about, really," Downson stated in his clipped speech. "You be at the spot when I sail in. I'll take over the bales. Pay you half its worth—remainder when I've turned it over. That big Negro chap of Madame Galante's will handle the labor end. Handsome woman, the Angelique. Had ideas there. No go. No! Bowled out each time I tried. But brainy. Good Lord, yes! Admire her. No end."

Haldane passed over the reference to Angelique, remarking that he couldn't understand why the money couldn't be handled as well by Big Indigo, as well as himself. Downson shook his head. "Prefer a white man," he stated shortly. "Had enough dealings to know. Africa. India. Other spots. Here and there. No depending on blacks. My word, no! This minute they're in a prime boil in Jamaica, over the new tax Governor

Eyre imposed. Mark what I say. There'll yet be trouble with those blacks down there. Not slaves, either. Free since 1834, y'know. That's it, Haldane. I prefer whites."

Haldane next asked regarding the necessary time for a trip to Jamaica, under sail. Downson shrugged lean shoulders. "Bit difficult to say, precisely. Some trips longer than others. *Perdita*'s just a small craft, y'know." He mentioned *Perdita*'s tonnage, which meant nothing at all to Haldane. "Schooner-rigged. Really too small to be termed a schooner, perhaps. Miniature model, what? Originally built as pleasure vessel. Owner's toy. Not commerce. But seaworthy. My word, yes! Quite, quite! A deal depends on weather we catch."

Downson mentioned prevailing winds, opposing winds, tides and currents, possible hurricanes. A stiff blow could create havoc with a sailing schedule. My word, yes! Or a prolonged calm. "Not like steam, y'know, Haldane. Sail's better, though. Cleaner. More sporting. Once in port it wants time to unload and restock. *Perdita*'s manned by a small crew. Three men. Myself. A harsh voyage means damaged rigging. That wants time for repairs. New equipment, perhaps. And there may be Yank ships to dodge. No telling. Busy beggars these days. They want cotton too. Y'see, difficult to say how long for a trip to Jamaic'."

They had another drink. Downson gave brief details of sailing in other parts, something of an ancient Viking spirit glowing in his keen eyes. The two maintained a pretense of the game, moving chessmen in rather desultory fashion about the checkered board. Downson abruptly arose. "It's settled then." Haldane got to his feet. "Monday night next, then, old man. Mme. Galante furnished complete instructions. I'll be there." He nodded, gave Haldane a firm grip from a rope-calloused hand, and departed. Haldane sat down again, thinking, savoring his absinthe. The sun was sinking when he stepped out to the *banquette*.

CHAPTER 11

Stars were glistening faintly overhead in a midnight sky of broken clouds, when Haldane and Taggert, in long coats and pulled-down hats passed through the hidden door in the wall at the rear of Maison Galante, and emerged via the succeeding courtyard on Bourbon Street, where Big Indigo waited with horses. The huge Negro, of a curious blue-black hue, possessed tremendous, muscular shoulders; his tones were slurred slightly with a French accent. He appeared a surprisingly gentle man. Haldane and Taggert mounted and he led the way out of New Orleans. Yellow-green gas jets sputtered on corner lamp posts along the narrow street, illuminating but little the few passers-by and the façades of closely built houses. In no time at all, it seemed, the riders reached open country where a fetid odor of swamps assailed their nostrils.

All night they rode through marshlands, Big Indigo pointing a circuitous course that provided the firmest footing for mounts. Gargantuan mosquitoes hovered in dense swarms over men and beasts. Gigantic cypress trees, moss-festooned, towered above. It was nearing three in the morning when Big Indigo commented, "Dis far, M'sieu Haldane, it was possible to bring de bales by wagon." Peering through the gloom, Haldane saw their course bordered a narrow estuary of bayou water, inky black in the faint light from the sky. "Here, de bales was moved to a barge and floated, roundabout, to de cotton-house. You can be glad we do not have to go dat long way."

Upon questioning, Big Indigo gave further information: he had been born of Haitian parents in New Orleans. He mentioned tenderly the many kindnesses of Arnaud Galante who had taken him in, while still an infant, at his parents' death from yellow fever, and had given him a certain education, and next work where he could learn all possible pertaining to the business of cotton. Then had come war, and the death of Arnaud Galante. Big Indigo fell silent. . . .

The horses splashed through shallow pools. A salmon dawn began to filter through overhanging cypress limbs. Presently the animals were belly-deep in sluggish swamp water; the riders lifted their booted feet from stirrups. Gradually, the way became more firm and open, though the footing still possessed a quaggy quality. They followed a grassy ridge tracing a meandering course through lower, wetter terrain. The horses crossed a brief sandy strip, then plunged again into swamp country. By this time the sun was up; Big Indigo produced from saddlebags bread, meat, and a flask of cold black coffee for breakfast.

They continued through somber, brooding

swamp country, tangled with vegetation. Moss-hung cypress trees like bearded patriarchs cast motionless reflections in stagnant pools of black water which was disturbed now and then when some slimy denizen of the murky slough slithered reluctantly from their path.

It was near noon when a series of sandy patches promised more solid going. A grove of live-oaks, with several loblolly pines rearing above, showed ahead. They wended a twisting way through the oaks and encountered undulating sand dunes. Then more oaks. Abruptly, through the trees, Haldane saw the blue waters of Breton Sound and heard the soft lapping of waves moving ceaselessly along sandy shores. Beyond lay a series of wooded islands. There was but little farther to go.

They found warm food awaiting them at the cotton-house, a long low structure of weathered cypress, extending toward the Sound, that blended well with closely surrounding trees and was completely hidden from view of any ship that might, possibly, risk the adjacent shallows. Two muscular Negroes in cotton pants and singlets had living quarters in a cleared space at the inland end of the building; the remainder of the structure was given over to racks on which were stacked the jute-covered bales of contraband cotton.

The remainder of the day passed quickly.

Haldane and Taggert strolled through the trees and arrived at a strip of grayish-white sand beach. Moored at one end was an unpainted, flat-bottomed barge, camouflaged with dead tree branches and piles of marsh grass. A growth of slanted reeds crowded along the shore. Haldane glanced across an expanse of sparkling sapphire water to the densely clustered low islands beyond, located so closely together that, from this distance, they afforded the appearance of a mainland.

Taggert eyed the undulating waters of the Sound, only a few fleecy clouds and a flight of screaming gulls distracting from the view. "Ain't a damn' boat in sight," he grumbled. "Like's not that Downson hombre won't ever show up, and even if he did show up, I don't see no channel where he could rein his boat through what you claim is islands. I told you right along I didn't like this and—"

Haldane interrupted to remind Taggert that Downson wasn't due until nightfall. They returned to the cotton-house to doze away the remainder of the day over brandy and cigars brought out by Big Indigo, until the call came for supper, prepared by the Negroes. Twilight came, lingered a few moments; darkness settled down. Accompanied by Haldane and Taggert, Big Indigo led the way to the shore, bearing a covered lantern in one hand. Some remaining light of day still lingered over the waters, but quickly vanished in the purple night. A star appeared and then, abruptly, the whole sky seemed dusted with tiny particles of light. It was yet too early for the moon. A soft whispering of gentle waves sounded continually along the shore. Big Indigo said presently, "M'sieu Downson comes, I think."

Haldane strained his eyes through the gloom. Just as he was about to tell the big Negro he was mistaken, that there wasn't a thing to be seen, the riding lights of a ship gleamed momentarily through sable darkness and then were instantly blotted from view. Big Indigo removed the cover from his lighted lantern and swung it briefly. Then the lantern was recovered and the circle of light in which the men stood, vanished. Haldane tensed a little, touching the butt of the cap-and-ball Colt's gun at his belt. If the arriving ship carried other than Downson and his crew . . .

From across the dark water the faint rasping of a muffled anchor chain interrupted his speculations. Five minutes passed. Ten. A slight squeaking of oarlocks reached Haldane's ears, and a skiff bearing three shadowy forms materialized from the gloom and nosed its way with a soft thud up the sandy beach. Haldane sensed, rather than saw, Downson's tall frame, followed by two other men, step from the skiff. Downson said quietly, "Pleasant night for sailing, y'know."

"With the right cargo," Haldane replied. They shook hands.

"Taggert, I presume?" Downson went on. Taggert said, "Damned if you didn't get here." He felt better after clasping Downson's hand.

Big Indigo led the way back to the cotton-house, only uncovering his lantern again, when they were once more among the trees. Haldane noted the heavy Colt's revolver at Downson's hip. Arriving at the cotton-house, they found brandy, cigars, food awaiting them on a bare pine table, which held also an oil lamp with a smoke-smudged chimney, lacking a globe. This stood at the inland end of the building. The tiers of baled cotton extended beyond. A draught of air swept through, and Haldane judged a door at the far end had been opened.

Downson finally gave orders to his two men and with Big Indigo assisting, the business of getting fifteen bales of cotton to the barge was commenced. "Look sharp, now, you blokes," Downson ordered. "No more showing of light than's wanted. There's a Federal gunboat cruising about, outside the islands. I intend to be clear as soon as possible."

A great amount of tugging, grunting and straining of muscles began at the far end of the cotton-house, where the first bales were being removed. Downson tossed on a table a small canvas sack that gave out a clinking sound as it landed. "Half the cash for fifteen bales, Mr. Haldane. Some gold and silver. Mostly U.S. bills. Count it if you like. Balance when I return from Jamaica." Haldane stated it wouldn't be necessary to count the money. As for returning to New Orleans with *Perdita*, would it be safe?

Downson stared his surprise. "Certainly, my dear fellow. Come and go as I please, y'know. Protection of Her British Majesty. Proper papers. That sort of thing. *Perdita* has to put in supplies, get outfitted, at New Orleans." He smiled cynically. "Not difficult to hoodwink the bloody Yanks. They imagine I sail for sport, y'know. Fishing in the Gulf. Hobby of marine life. That sort of balderdash. My word, yes!"

They applied themselves to the bottle and cigars. Downson talked steadily under the spell of smooth brandy, of Chinese pirates, gun running, and various other adventures, until Taggert's eyes bulged from their sockets. The time passed quickly while the cotton was being loaded aboard *Perdita*. Almost before he realized it, Haldane had said good-bye to Downson and was once more climbing into his saddle, with Taggert and Big Indigo at his side.

The following evening, when Angelique Galante handed him his share of the revenue from the cotton shipment, Haldane asserted that his earning of the money had been almost too easy. He repeated the words to Taggert, later, while dividing the money, and Taggert, at first mollified by sight of the cash, frowned suddenly. "That's exactly what I don't like about this business, Garth. It's almost too easy. I never knew of no good to come from money that wa'n't sweated for."

CHAPTER 12

Twice more before the year 1865 was ended, Garth Haldane went through the simple (to him) business of contacting Rupert Downson at the cotton-house and receiving in exchange for a certain number of bales of cotton, the canvas sack of money. There had been various delays. A revolt of Negroes at Morant Bay, with its resultant murdering of whites, while it had been quelled, had left Jamaica in a rather precarious position; labor was uncertain to come by. There had been other annoying incidents to retard Downson's movements. Time had been expended in seeking the highest possible price for the contraband bales. Only on the first delivery had it been possible to get one dollar the pound. Later, the market had fluctuated between seventy-five and ninety-two cents. Even at that price, as Taggert put it, they were doing "plumb elegant." Draughts for the money they received had been forwarded to Haldane's bank in San Antonio.

Despite the drop in price, Angelique Galante was well satisfied. Downson had been prompt in remitting moneys owed. Haldane, however, grew restive. There was building in him a definite yearning for White Hawk Acres; he was eager to begin reconstruction, though privately he conceded that his none-too-frequent contacts with Angelique had a tendency to retire his thoughts of home momentarily to the background. But Angelique's gaming *salon*, which Haldane hadn't again visited, occupied her evenings; during the day she was rarely to be seen, except when the business of cotton, or an occasional invitation to dine, brought about meetings. She was extremely business-like and when Haldane pointed out she was furnishing beds and lodging for himself and men, and insisted on paying for what they received, she had, with true Gallic thrift, raised no objections. It would mean more money for the cause.

The truth was, Garth Haldane told himself, easy living and comfortable surroundings could become irksome. It was lack of activity that galled; that and a persistent grumbling on Taggert's part regarding the delay in reaching Texas. Lustrous alone appeared entirely satisfied. With nourishing food and proper rest he had lost much of his scrawny appearance.

It was early in February before Rupert Downson was next heard from: he had been delayed by a storm that had necessitated a new sail and other refitting: Downson named the date on which he was prepared to meet Haldane and arrange another shipment of cotton bales. The Englishman's messages, reaching Angelique by some circuitous, underground route, were always terse, and interested Haldane but little, beyond the announcement of the next meeting date at the cotton-house. As usual, with Judd Taggert and Big Indigo, he rode on the appointed evening to carry out the assignment.

Two nights later they returned, soaked to the hips in swamp water. "I knowed it, I knowed it, I knowed somethin' was bound to happen," Taggert kept saying, as he and Haldane dragged their weary steps across the moon-flooded courtyard. "Like I been maintainin' right along, it was too easy to be safe, and even if it was safe, I ain't never yet got used to runnin' from Yank bastuds—"

"It's not necessary you repeat what you've already said, Judd," Haldane protested wearily. "Let's get to bed and thrash things out tomorrow." Mounting the stairway to the balcony, Haldane glanced across the courtyard and was surprised to note the windows of the gaming *salon* were dark. It wasn't yet midnight. Taggert interrupted Haldane's ominous speculations with the remark that he intended to get drunk and sleep all day tomorrow. They could thrash things out the day after. Lustrous and Robert had come hurrying up after them with word that hot water for baths would be arranged immediately. Taggert reached his room, entered and angrily slammed the door.

Haldane was stepping from his bath, considerably refreshed by the hot water and a tumbler of cognac, and dwelling on certain matters mentioned by Lustrous, when a knock sounded at his door. Lustrous went to answer it, and returned with word that Mme. Galante wished to confer with Major Haldane as soon as possible. Haldane dressed carefully and presented himself at Angelique's door, which was opened by Babet. Within burned a single shaded light. Babet explained he was to proceed to the inner chamber; there had been an annoyance; madame suffered from an aching of the head. If M'sieu would please to follow . . . The little mulatto maid gave him a final amused glance from dusky, mischievous eyes, as she left him at the entrance to Angelique Galante's boudoir. He heard Angelique's invitation to enter and her final instructions to Babet. "For tonight, that is all, Babet."

The room Haldane had entered was almost as large as the one through which he had just passed. There were the same high plastered walls and fan-shaped draped windows. Angelique in a long-sleeved white dressing gown, trimmed with a great deal of frilly lace, sat before a fireplace with a sculptured Carrara marble mantel. Her knees were crossed and Haldane saw she wore on her slim bare feet a pair of ivory-hued *nonchalantes* enriched with braid the color of burnt sienna. A suffusion of shining chestnut hair, caught with a white ribbon, flowed across the cushion placed between her head and the high back of the deep chair.

Cypress logs in the fireplace dispelled the evening's damp air, their dancing flames captured in the polished doors of a rosewood armoire, which in turn reflected gleams of flickering light in the oval mirror of a dressing table, draped on either side with ivory satin. A wide Seignouret bed occupied one corner, the pillows and yellow silk coverlet holding the recent impression of Angelique's rounded form. A small table stood near the bed, bearing a single lighted candlestick casting its illumination over an open account book. A second high-back chair stood near Angelique's; between the two was placed a low octagonal table of San Domingo mahogany with a marble top, holding a seven-branched candelabrum and a tray arranged with sliced cold fowl, bread, cheese and wine. A carpet of soft brown left a wide border of parquetry floor showing. An interior, Garth Haldane mused, reflecting a certain distinction, an air of elegance.

Angelique lifted one arm in a sweeping gesture. "You find an admiration for my room, M'sieu Haldane?" Haldane apologized for his preoccupation and assured her the room was a perfect symphony of browns, yellows and ivory, in which she herself provided the harmony, the dominating theme. "Ah, ever the very deep South, M'sieu. Eternally." Again he was conscious of her dimples. "Tonight, M'sieu, I confess a mood for such fine-spoken words. Sit, please. I shall not even offer an apology for asking you in here. But, earlier, I was indisposed."

Seating himself next to the low table that adjoined her chair, Haldane remarked that in other women headaches generally resulted in an impairment of charm that was immediately manifest, whereas with Mme. Galante, the exact contrary was to be observed. Her teeth, he mused, were very white and even when she smiled.

"My headache! *Pouf*! It has long since departed, being not the ache of an illness, but one brought about by an extreme anger. That, and a certain concern that you did not return as soon as expected." Haldane replied he'd explain in a minute; meanwhile, Lustrous had mentioned a visit of Colonel Albro Isham and two infantrymen to Maison Galante.

Instantly, crimson spots of anger rose to Angelique's white cheeks. "Soldiers! *Ah, diable*! This Colonel Isham will yet prove the death of me. The beastly swine! To him, M'sieu Haldane, I have paid more than nine thousands of dollars since he arranges the permission to reopen my gaming *salon*. I will demonstrate!" She came abruptly out of her chair in a swirling of foamy lace that revealed momentarily a rounded white knee and slim ankle, diffusing a delicate fragrance of vetiver to Haldane's nostrils, as she stormed across the room, to return an instant later with the open account book which was plumped down on Haldane's lap. Reaching over his shoulder, she riffled the pages feverishly, indicating with a trembling forefinger, certain penned numerals. "You see? Here and here and here! These amounts I have paid out to this fat Colonel Albro Isham!" Her voice, her whole form, shook with rage, and a torrent of shining chestnut hair, loosened from its ribbon, and enveloped both Haldane and the ledger in an aromatic cloud which he found not unpleasant.

Sleeves slipped back from bare rounded arms as they lifted to recapture the chestnut tresses, nimble fingers quickly retying the white ribbon. Snatching the account book from his lap, she flung it furiously across the room where it landed on the bed.

Haldane viewed her flashing eyes and heaving breast with some amusement, of which Angelique gradually became aware. Abruptly, she whirled away and plopped angrily into her chair where she sat glaring at him, until the resentment in her face had been replaced by a rueful smile. "*Sacre bleu*! I behave like one insane. You will pardon, M'sieu? It is not frequent I experience a losing of the temper. It comes of an effect this Colonel Isham has on me. Always! And never am I entirely free of thought of him. I feel, always, as though he were just behind me with his probings eternal, ready to pounce. But enough of such a specimen." She indicated the food on the table. "It occurred to one this might be welcome on your return." Haldane thanked her and expressed a wish to learn more of Colonel Isham's visit.

She nibbled daintily on a small slice of chicken breast while she talked. "No, it was not more money from the gaming—not entirely this time— he demanded. Again it is the cotton. He insists I possess hidden bales. I swore it was not true. You see how this Colonel Isham persists to make a liar of me? Next he mentions a duel of which he has heard, between a Yankee captain, named Gratton, and some Englishman who, he claims, has frequented Maison Galante. Of this, I have no knowledge, of course. He knows nothing of a certainty, M'sieu Haldane. He only probes and probes, hoping I will some place make the slip.

"I offer a suggestion he consult Captain Gratton. Reluctantly, Colonel Isham admits he does not know this Gratton's whereabouts, and Gratton's papers have been found not all they should be. This Gratton has vanished, leaving no trace. Next I tell this porcine Isham, 'If an Englishman is involved, request information of the British Consulate.' That I know he would not do. The Consulate would look down his long cold nose at Colonel Isham, and make the suggestion Colonel Isham make inquiries through proper government channels at Washington. *Non*! He will learn exactly nothing from the British Consulate. So, this subject was also dropped."

Haldane put down his glass of Meursault and retrieved from a plate of thin porcelain a sliver of cheese. He understood, he said, there had been a search made of the house. Mme. Galante nodded vehement agreement. "It is true! Colonel Isham states it is rumored a white man lives here. You see, more of his probing? Had he known anything of a verity he would have mentioned *two* men."

Her laugh made music in the room. "It was an insult he offered me, with such talk. Me, I fly from my handle. Does he think me a *cocotte*? I indulged in a scene of the most dramatic, instantly turning out all players and closing my gaming *salon. Helas*! I experienced a swooning, and while prone on the sofa, whispered to Babet a swift message. She departed on the instant to see to the concealment of your effects. And M'sieu Taggert's. I wept! Ah, M'sieu Haldane, I wept most beautifully. It was of a complete convincing."

She paused and a tiny reminiscent frown gathered above her dark eyes. "Or was it? . . . By this time, Colonel Albro Isham becomes uncertain, at least. I insist for the sake of my honor, my unsullied reputation, that he make a searching through Maison Galante for this rumored white man. I demand this searching! He was reluctant—I think—and sent the two *soldats*.

When they return, they bring the report there is to be found no evidence of such a man on my premises. I rise to my feet. I make a dramatic pointing of the finger. I order from my door, Colonel Albro Isham. I swear I shall never again open Maison Galante. He begs that I reconsider. *Zut*! I recommend him to the devil." She looked uncertainly at Haldane. "You decide I am a hussy, *n'est-ce pas*?"

His lips twitching, Garth Haldane assured Angelique Galante he considered her far from a hussy. She brightened instantly. "But a hussy I am, nonetheless, M'sieu. But, what would you?" A Gallic shrugging of white lace shoulders beneath burnished chestnut hair. "This Colonel Isham is of the most revolting. He apologizes of the most fervent. Almost he goes to the knees. Ah, *le cochon gros*! *Le coquin*! Imagine if you can a fat pig on the knees! And so he took the departure. The gaming *salon* will remain closed one week. It will teach him to make no more of these probings. But what an experience! It gave my head to ache. Of a verity!"

The scorn in her eyes gradually faded and Haldane saw she was still a little frightened, not entirely free of the ominous shadow the wily Colonel Isham had cast over Maison Galante. An instinctive urge to gather her in his arms and quiet her fears possessed Haldane. "But, M'sieu Haldane, he is shrewd. There exists a brain behind those small swine eyes. *Rendre justice au diable*. I give that devil his due. Always I have the feeling he is closing in. It will be of much relief when the cotton-house is emptied. And then I shall tell Colonel Isham—*Mon Dieu*! Such a giving out of words. I afford you no opportunity to explain why your return was delayed."

Haldane placed on the table a small canvas sack that gave off dull clinking sounds. "The usual half," he said, and went on: yes, there'd been some trouble. The cotton bales had been shipped aboard *Perdita* as customary, he had said good-bye to Rupert Downson and accompanied by Taggert and Big Indigo, commenced the return journey to New Orleans.

An hour's ride from the cotton-house, they had heard what sounded like the firing of ship's cannon, out on the waters of Breton Sound. "If *Perdita* was involved, I naturally have no way of knowing. Downson had informed me there's been considerable cruising about of U.S. gunboats on the look-out for smugglers, gun runners and the like. According to him, it's this Emperor Maximilian business in Mexico has Washington worried. That's why all Louisiana ports have been closed to traffic with Mexico. It's possible of course Downson wasn't involved with the firing we heard. On the other hand, the Federals may have been after him. I simply don't know. Judd, Big Indigo, and I continued on, hoping for the best. Thirty minutes later when we were rounding the bank of a bayou, in full moonlight, we were hailed by a detachment of eight Yank cavalrymen who called on us to halt."

"And you make of the refusal?" Angelique's dark eyes were wide.

Haldane nodded. "With the papers Judd and I carried, we *might* have bluffed our way out, but I was uncertain if they'd accept Judd as an Englishman. And it would have been difficult explaining our presence in the swamp. And so,"—drawing a weary reminiscent breath—"we made a run for it, Big Indigo showing the way. When they started shooting, we were forced to reply in like fashion."

"You killed them?"—quick eager tones.

"I don't know," Haldane replied slowly. "I saw two drop from saddles. A third slumped as though he were badly hurt. We didn't wait to learn the outcome." He continued: with Taggert and Big Indigo he had sought concealment among the deep swamp cypress. At least five of the Yanks had doggedly pursued the trail until dawn had come and the day was well on to noon, before Big Indigo's ingenious twistings and turnings had eluded the pursuers. It was a problem whether or not the Yanks would ever find their way out.

"Big Indigo was marvelous, a man to tie to. I wonder if anyone knows the swamps better. At times we swam water over the horses' depth, but always he brought us to solid footing again. We considered making a stand and fighting the Yanks off, but they were armed with Spencer repeating rifles. Judd and I had only our six-shooters. Big Indigo was unarmed. I'm quite sure we could have handled them, but it was a risk I didn't want to take. You see, it's not like a real war"—he was very earnest about this, insisting she should completely understand—"we had to make sure of coming back to be on hand for the remaining shipments of your cotton, and—"

"Damn this cotton!" Angelique burst out.

He continued as though he hadn't heard her, "—and so we turned tail, ran for it, shook them off and got clear. It was the running away that got Judd mad. I can't say I disagree with him, though it was no doubt necessary."

The color had left Angelique's face. She rose and commenced nervously pacing the room. "This Colonel Albro Isham will yet cause us a great deal of trouble," she insisted in choked tones. Haldane wondered if Isham were concerned in the business. "*Mais oui*! I think there is small doubt. He has a determination to find my cotton, you comprehend? He maintains patrols in the swamps in hope of intercepting us. As to this gunboat, no. I do not think that was of his doing. That would bring involvement with the U.S. Navy. He dares not include too many in his little schemes. If a few of his underlings get killed, he cares"—she snapped her fingers—"not so much. He has the heart of a mustard-seed size. He is—" Angelique paused, eyes widening suddenly at thought of another contingency; she halted her pacing before him. "M'sieu Haldane! It is *you* who might have been killed!"

That, Haldane told her in an even voice, was a possibility deserving slight consideration. He had been shot at a great deal during the past four years, he pointed out with some humor, and hadn't yet been killed. Besides, he reminded her, that was a potentiality allowed for when he and Madame Galante had made their bargain.

"But I did not understand all it would mean," Angelique protested earnestly. "Never did I think there would be such a shooting. In my mind was only a fooling of the Yankees, of snatching from under his pig snout the cotton Colonel Isham tries so hard to find. Then, I planned, when the last bale was on the voyage to Jamaica, and we had the money, you and I, I planned to laugh in his face of *le cochon*. Of a verity! You believe me, M'sieu?"

She dropped insistently on her knees at the side of his chair, her dark eyes moist, and he became intensely aware of the provocative fragrance of vetiver. No, he told her quietly, he couldn't quite think she believed herself. After living these past years under the Federal boot in an occupied New Orleans and doing the things she had done, surely she wasn't so naïve as to think she could flaunt Yankee authority with impunity; shooting affrays were almost certain, if not worse, any time Yankee displeasure was incurred. Certainly she should be aware of that fact.

"Perhaps," Angelique conceded reluctantly, "you speak truth. It is possible I see differently tonight on such matters. Something, it may be, has opened my eyes. But it is still not too late to make the change in our plans. There will be no more shipping of cotton. This Colonel Isham may have all that is left, if he can find it. I will not have you risk death from the shooting—"

Haldane interrupted a trifle harshly with a contradiction, maintaining it was too late to turn back. "I've passed my word. To you. To Rupert Downson. He trusts in us. I promised to remain in New Orleans until every last bale had left. We can't stop now. Do you want to give in to the Yankees? At any rate, I don't intend to let you. Had you been hounded through that swamp as we were, you might realize how I feel and know how bitter defeat can taste."

A great weariness swept over him, his legs ached as a rankling memory of the fight enveloped his thoughts. His manner softened when she confessed in a rather subdued voice that she disliked, as much as he, capitulating to Yankee greed. But it was only that she disliked still more the thought of him being shot at, getting killed. Still kneeling at the side of his chair, she gazed up at him.

Haldane's eyes went to the white hand resting on the arm of his chair, his gaze ranged slowly upward, seeing the firm curve of swelling breasts in the lacy opening at her throat, pausing a moment on the slightly-parted full red lips, before he perceived the anxiety in her eyes. How had that poet phrased it: fathomless dark pools limpid with an ageless joy? She glanced away and the movement of her head diffused a perfumed aura from the thick strands of chestnut. Fathomless dark pools . . . A kind of chaos seized on Haldane's consciousness, and he heard himself saying, as though from far away, in a somewhat unsteady voice, that it was well past the time when he should be bidding her good-night.

"Is it necessary, M'sieu Garth Haldane?" Angelique asked quietly. "Is it necessary that you make your departure so soon?"

He rose deliberately from the chair and moved about the room, snuffing out the guttering candles and drawing back the drapes from the tall, fan-shaped windows. Moonlight laved the room in liquid silver, leaving to the flickering flames of cypress logs in the fireplace only the task of reaching the darkest corners. He approached the kneeling figure near the chair and when she rose to meet him, a fragrance of vetiver mounted to his throat and nostrils, thickening his tones, as he told her that though there were a great many things necessary in this world, leaving her now, at this moment, was not one of them.

CHAPTER 13

Three days later—it was nearly noon—Haldane found Angelique at breakfast in her sitting room. Beyond, Babet's movements in the bedroom attested Angelique's late rising. She was at the table in a dressing gown of pale burnt-sienna, chestnut hair piled high on her shapely head, consuming the last of an omelet. Her eyes lighted when he entered. "Garth! You appear to have been awake for hours. You have breakfasted, *n'est-ce pas*?"

Haldane assured her he had eaten some time since, and started to change the subject when she interrupted: "To judge from the look of your face, you are to be of the most serious this morning. For such as that, it is too early. Of a verity! *Tiens*! Kiss me and I shall award you with a cup of coffee. Perhaps, if the kiss is a very nice one, you shall have two cups."

Her voice was gay and the pleasant gleam of silver and china on spotless linen, gave him pause. He came to her, as her arms lifted to him, tightening warmly about his shoulders. A minute passed before she gently pushed him away, a mock reprimand in her eyes. He mentioned something having to do with her loveliness increasing each time he saw her. "It is,

Garth, perhaps you who gets the credit for that. Nonetheless, that compliment was not up to your standard, beloved. It is plain you are not of the very deep South, this morning. You have a thing on your mind. Sit, *s'il vous plait.*"

He accepted a chair at her side, while she poured black coffee and lighted one of her slim cigars. "Now, M'sieu Garth Haldane," she said submissively, "one is prepared to learn what brings to your face so much of a gravity."

Haldane drew from his pocket a folded copy of *L'Abeille* and spread it before her. "This blasted newspaper," he explained irritably, "contains something about a Federal gunboat running aground in Breton Sound, which may have something to do with the firing we heard the other night. But I read French but poorly, and I can not quite—"

"But, Garth, you did not know there is also published, *simultanement*, the translation in English. I will tell Robert to hereafter procure it for you. Either that, or"—her dimples deepened— "you must learn French. Of a certainty. There is in all the world no language like the French for making love. Of that I assure you. . . . Enough! Let us to this business of the gunboat."

The dark eyes widened excitedly as she scanned the article, commencing to read aloud in rippling French. Haldane finally managed to make her understand it was an English translation he sought. "Of a verity! The English arrives, *tout de suite*!" More slowly now: "It states here in letters of a black size, 'U.S. Gunboat Aground. Chase of Mysterious Ship—'" Followed voluble French intersprinkled with English, in which Haldane distinguished the words "escaping schooner" and "gunfire." Abruptly, Angelique put down the paper, her eyes serious. "Is it that you believe M'sieu Downson is spoken of?"

That, Haldane informed her, was a subject on which he had no opinion, whatever. He hadn't, so far, been able to make much sense of what she'd read, and if it did pertain to Downson in any way, it was important to know what *L'Abeille* offered. Would she, he asked dryly, please forget the translation and relate in her own sweet words, *in English,* such information as the paper gave?

"I am so sorry, Garth," Angelique said humbly. "It was the excitement of this that I read that makes me not to think. I offer what it tells here"—indicating the newspaper—"of the Federal gunboat *Tonawanda*, and of how this *Tonawanda* sights in the moonlight—Garth, the identical night you heard the shooting!—a small schooner slipping between the islands of Breton Sound. The *Tonawanda* hails this small schooner, demanding of her in the name of the U.S. Government that she come about, make the halt, *a l'instant*, but the schooner only makes to flee the faster. Thinking it possible the schooner runs guns to Maximilian, in Mexico, the *Tonawanda* opens with a cannonfire, and it is thought one mast of the schooner was brought down, but that is not certain, as the small ship continued to flight until it is lost to view behind an island.

"The *Tonawanda* pursued the search and one half hour later sees again the schooner, sneaking to the shelter of another island. There ensues further firing of the cannon. But with so many islands, the ship makes the escape. And of a sudden, *avec precipitation*, this *Tonawanda* finds the schooner has led it to a spot of shallows, where she is stuck on the bottom, between two islands. Daylight arrives by the time the *Tonawanda* is free to once more move, but now the small schooner has made of a complete vanishing." Angelique's eyes were wide. "You consider, Garth, that the small ship is Rupert Downson's *Perdita*?"

Frowning, Haldane replied that he feared so. Angelique nodded vigorously. "I think there is no doubt. And M'sieu Downson made the escape clean. Of a certainty. Otherwise we should have had word from him." Haldane said dubiously he hoped so, and asked if there were anything in the paper relative to his meeting with Yankee cavalry in the swamp. Angelique searched through *L'Abeille* and shook her head. "I did not imagine there would be. That was of Colonel Isham's doings, and he will make no mention of such for fear something may be learned of his black plannings."

"Well," Haldane sighed, "there is nothing to do now but hope for word from Rupert Downson."

"Nothing at all, my Garth?" Angelique asked meaningly. Haldane smilingly advised her not to take him too literally. He considered, he informed her, engaging in the study of the French language to pass time; perhaps, she'd be willing to tutor him. Angelique dimpled; that which he mentioned was an *idee* of a marvelous perfection. He would see, M'sieu Garth Haldane, with what an incredible swiftness would come his education under her tutelage.

During April, a letter and a bank draught covering the sale of cotton, arrived from Rupert Downson by English steamship to New Orleans, thence, via the grapevine, to Angelique. Perhaps, Downson wrote, they had heard something of his brush with a Federal gunboat, *Tonawanda*; he had since learned the gunboat had gone aground in Breton Sound that night, fortunately for him and *Perdita*. Though flying British colors, Downson explained, he had had no proper clearance papers for cotton, and had thought it best to show a clean pair of heels when ordered by the *Tonawanda* to halt, rather than involve Her Majesty's government. Thereupon the gunboat had opened fire.

The damage to *Perdita* had been considerable; Downson, himself, had suffered a broken arm from a falling mast; one of the schooner's crew had been killed outright. Only now the broken arm showed signs of healing. The *Perdita* had managed with difficulty to escape; it had been necessary to rig a jury mast to maintain way. Leaks had complicated matters. For a time, Downson had thought it impossible to stay afloat in the Gulf. Luckily, a passing British vessel, bound for Jamaica, had taken the schooner in tow and given other requisite aid until port was raised. The *Perdita* would require a great deal of overhauling before she could again set sail. However, certain cabins built for pleasure sailing, were being knocked out, and from now on *Perdita* would be able to carry a greater cargo than formerly. Downson closed with word he would return to America sometime in July, at which date, both injured arm and damaged ship would again be in commission; an earlier arrival was definitely impossible. July! Haldane shrugged and was content.

The news, however, was received with consternation by Judd Taggert, who swore that Texas seemed farther away all the time. "Our getting west of yesterday," he grumbled, "seems to have bogged down."

Surprisingly, the days passed more swiftly than anticipated. Haldane had begun to study French and was laboriously translating into English a copy of Voltaire's *Zadig*. The weeks, months, slipped by. Lacking the accustomed daily exercise in the saddle, Haldane went to fence three days a week, with a Spanish master who maintained an academy on Conti Street. He spent frequent evenings with Angelique, such time as she wasn't occupied with her gaming *salon*, though since its reopening she had largely turned the management over to her head croupier, Edouard Janvier, who for years had manipulated the roulette wheel for the elder Galante. Haldane had an impression that Edouard Janvier disliked him, though the thin-lipped, bleak-eyed croupier always addressed him with the utmost courtesy when they met. Which was infrequently. Still, Haldane never quite trusted Janvier.

Even Taggert became reconciled to the delay when an interest in cock-fighting suddenly possessed him, and he attended various cocking mains held in New Orleans, though each time he left the house, Haldane was uneasy until his return. The sergeant even indulged his hobby to the extent of purchasing two gamecocks, a Dominique and a Claiborne, thereafter spending much time in the courtyard trimming wings at a proper slope, cutting down tails and otherwise preparing and training his birds.

Occasionally, he and Haldane emerged at night (leaving always by the secret walled door at rear) to walk about the city, though they found little entertainment to their taste. Life for white citizens of New Orleans had become increasingly difficult the business of adjusting to a life of equality with the Negro came hard. Fighting in the streets was a nightly occurrence; violence and thieving prevailed. Lustrous Candent appeared content. The daily shaving, and caring for Haldane's clothing, constituted almost his sole duties; he enjoyed the companionship of the other servants.

It was a day in June when Haldane found Angelique one morning at breakfast. He kissed her, made proper compliments on her appearance. The dressing gown, this morning, was of a pale yellowish green—the color of absinthe, he decided. She indicated a chair, poured coffee, and shoved across the table a Ch'ien Lung compote of jumbal biscuits, a favorite tidbit of his, without speaking. She appeared distressed. He asked what was wrong. She mentioned Colonel Albro Isham.

"Has that Yankee tyrant been here again?"

Angelique shook her head. "But all of yesterday afternoon two men spied on Maison Galante, from across Dauphine Street, to learn who arrives and departs. *Soldats* in blue uniforms, also, stood near. I watched from a window. Colonel Isham comes once, talks to them, departs. I feel always he arranges to close in"—she shuddered—"and I experience a terror. Garth, you will not let him come near me?"

"Not if I can stop him. Perhaps I shall some day. Are his men out there now?"

"As yet I have not perceived them. They may not appear. That pig devil manages always to do that which one cannot foresee. He is like a thing horrible, crawling sluggishly, but surely, from beneath slimy rocks, to spread and envelop one—"

"Angelique, my dear. Don't let it shake you so. So far you have been more than a match for him—"

"It is only of the temporary, Garth. This will pass. I fear not so much for myself. But for you, an unsurrendered Confederate officer . . ." She broke off, shivering.

"This is nonsense," he said earnestly. "You're just in low spirits this morning. Perhaps I may prescribe a little brandy?"

She didn't reply, but sat turning the jade ring upon her finger. Slowly, she drew it off, studying the Chinese symbols carved in the stone: the *chou*, a symbol of longevity; the bat and peach so intricately cut, with a bit of crimson in the jade forming the bloom on the peach. Her shoulders lifted hopelessly. "Long life, happiness, wealth— *zut*! This is not for me." Impulsively, "Garth, it would please me for you to accept this ring." She pushed it across the table.

Haldane protested, but when he realized the acceptance would please her, he ceased arguing.

To his surprise, it fitted the little finger of his left hand. She brushed aside his thanks. "You have strong fingers, but slim, my Garth. I had the impression my ring would fit." Momentarily, her customary gaiety returned, her dark eyes sparkled. "So! You have not given me a ring. *Au contraire*! I give to you the ring. A reverse of custom, *n'est-ce pas*? It is a symbol of what we have been to each other."

"*Have* been?" he queried, and started to say more.

"Do not say 'forever,'" she warned quickly. "It is a word that comes too easily to men's lips. Me, Angelique Galante, I make no demand for promises. If I find happiness in the present, it is all that makes count. Garth, always you will find some woman to care for you. If not me, someone else. But, on occasion, you will look at that ring, and you will remember me then."

"Angelique, you are in a queer mood. I'm not sure I—"

"*Tiens*!" she was suddenly laughing. "Forget what I say, Garth. You think I have an attack of the woman's vapors, no? As you say, it is a mood. And now I shall determine if you are to be made jealous. Last night, I had the proposal."

"Proposal? What sort of proposal?" He frowned.

"A proposal of marriage. What other type should make interest for a woman? It is Edouard Janvier who desires my hand in marriage."

"Janvier?" He remembered then, the bleak-featured croupier of the roulette wheel. "Oh, yes"—wryly. "At any rate, he is to be congratulated on his good taste. He appreciates—"

"That cold fish!" Her short laugh was almost a snort. "Edouard Janvier appreciates nothing but money. It is that he proposes a marriage of convenience, an arrangement of business only."

Haldane ventured a question: so long as this Janvier was so familiar with Maison Galante activities, did he have any—er—suspicions as regarded the relations existing between Angelique and Garth Haldane?

Angelique gave a toss of the chestnut hair, shrugged shapely shoulders. "He may, or may not, have such a suspicion. This much I do not care"—her snapping fingers made a sharp noise—"nor would it matter greatly to Edouard Janvier if he knew. To him, love is nothing. Money only matters. And if, through marriage, he gains control of Maison Galante, that is his sole interest. You have heard, Garth, that these Yankees have a greed for money. Janvier is far worse."

Haldane suddenly remembered her previous marriage. "But what of Achille—you are married to him—even in France—?"

"Have I not told you? Two weeks since, I have this letter from Achille Lavache, stating he has arranged an annulment of our marriage.

Doubtless he has found one with money. I think, also, he has had a contact with Edouard Janvier. That Janvier was most pressing."

"And what did you tell Edouard Janvier?" Haldane asked, amused.

"I gave M'sieu Janvier advice of the most excellent, telling him to return to his roulette and roll his little ball. He was overcome with a rage. Of a verity! But I know Edouard. He will try again."

She poured more coffee, and lighted a slim cigar, putting it down again after only a couple of puffs. "You feel it queer I did not before tell you about Achille Lavache? The matter slipped my mind. It was of small consequence. Think nothing of it. He was never a husband, except on papers legal. Of another letter I remember now to tell you. Laure Gabriel will be passing through New Orleans. You will remember her?"

"Laure!" Haldane's face lighted. "I'll never forget that girl. I'm still under deep obligation. Where is she going? When will she arrive here?"

"*Parbleu*! my Garth! One could almost imagine you have an infatuation for this girl." Angelique laughed at Haldane's heightened color. "Ah, *mon Dieu*, I do but jest. When Laure arrives is of an uncertainty. As one of our agents, her work is finished in the east. In Texas, where the Federal Government plans much deviltry, she will prove useful. At a town named Bandera, where she has relatives. Do you know of this Bandera?"

"Bandera? Great Scott! If I were home at White Hawk Acres, we'd practically be neighbors. It's not far from San Antonio."

"*Tres bien*! You may yet, once more, work together against these accursed Yankee thieves. In her letter she asked, not wishing to travel alone into that strange Texas, if I could provide a man, a servant, to accompany her. At once, I thought of your man, Lustrous—Candent, is the name?—who wishes also to return to Texas. I thought, if you have no objection—"

"The very thing, Angelique. It will please Lustrous, too, and get him home that much the sooner. It will be fine to see Laure, again."

Angelique eyed him shrewdly. "Garth, you do show an interest. I think, perhaps, Laure Gabriel might make you the good wife." Haldane, color lifting, stated that Angelique Galante was his only interest where women were concerned. "Ah, my Garth," she laughed, "that is very nicely said, and because it is nice, I'll forgive you that small lie. When Lustrous leaves, I shall tell Robert to appoint you another man to do for you."

"My thanks. I'll speak to Lustrous. Judd, too. Judd thought a lot of Laure."

"It is arranged then." Haldane nodded that it was, and advised her to stop worrying about Colonel Isham, that all would work out all right, though privately he wasn't so sure of it.

As he strolled slowly back around the balcony to his room, he glanced at the jade ring on his finger. What was it Angelique had said? Oh, yes . . . "you will look at that ring and remember me then." Remember me, then. Where had he heard those words before? . . . remember me, then. Abruptly, memory's fingers turned over a picture in his mind, a picture of a girl with corn-silk hair, declaiming something from Byron, ending, ". . . remember me, then." The last words he had heard Laure Gabriel speak when they were leaving the Boar & Tankard Inn. Laure . . . cornflower blue eyes . . .

Frowning, he continued on into his room.

CHAPTER 14

July arrived, hot and muggy, augmenting a confused impatience that had been slowly growing in Haldane. Big Indigo had been coming in each week from the cotton-house to learn if any word had been had from Rupert Downson; he, too, had begun to fret over the delayed shipment of bales. The Yankees were tightening their control on the city daily; Big Indigo felt trouble was due to break. But there was nothing to do but mark time. A letter had been received from Downson; he hoped to set sail shortly for New Orleans. Somewhat relieved, Big Indigo headed back through the swamp; he would return to Maison Galante within a few days.

Haldane was seated one afternoon in the courtyard, endeavouring to foil the heat with a long cold drink and a palmetto fan. From his glass the scent of rum and limes rose to his nostrils. Glancing up at a slight sound, Haldane saw a door flung back from the gaming *salon*, and there emerged on the balcony a hard-faced man with sleek hair like a polished boot. Haldane frowned, then recognized Edouard Janvier, the head croupier.

As Janvier flung himself angrily down the stairway to the courtyard, without perceiving

Haldane who sat partly concealed by a hanging leaf of a tubbed banana tree, Haldane wondered what was up. Angelique's croupiers didn't generally put in an appearance until darkness had fallen. The croupier disappeared through the great doors to the street, leaving one of them standing ajar. Rather than bother a servant, Haldane crossed the courtyard and closed it himself, then returned to his seat.

Angelique descended from the balcony presently. Haldane called to her and she crossed to sit at his side, first asking permission to have a drink from his glass. Her face was white with anger, the chestnut hair somewhat loosened. "That Edouard!" she exclaimed. Haldane asked if she referred to her croupier. Angelique nodded violently. "Who else but Edouard Janvier should place me in such a state? I had made a demand that he come today to examine with me the accounts. It is unbelievable! *Le coquin*! Consider, my Garth, it was my father, years ago, who lifted him from the gutter and taught him to operate the wheel. And now, this M'sieu Janvier—this imbecile, this thief, this specimen!—is not to be trusted with the money of the daughter." She burst into heated French, too fast for Haldane to follow, but he gathered, after a time, that Edouard Janvier had been feathering his own nest from the proceeds of the gaming *salon*.

"*Mon Dieu*, Garth! What is there to do? I have given him his *congé*, his discharge. The stolen money he may retain. And would you believe? It is this same M'sieu Janvier who makes to me the proposal of marriage! Ah, never again will I trust any man. They are not to be trusted—"

Haldane laughed and asked, "Shall I order up my horse and leave?"

She smiled suddenly. "Is it that you believe I class you with other men, my Garth? *Non, grace a Dieu*!" Again, she flamed and stamped a small foot. "But I appeal to you. Is it not of a most detestable?"

Haldane agreed; he wondered, however, regarding the problematical results of such an abrupt dismissal. Janvier was, after all, thoroughly cognizant of Angelique's underground dealings during the war and since. Did he know of the hidden cotton-house? Angelique pursed her lips, frowned, and nodded. "He is aware I some place possess hidden bales. He was present when they were removed from Maison Galante. But he has no knowledge of the place we hide them."

Haldane mentioned a possibility of Janvier making trouble for her. "*Oui*, Garth, it is possible," she admitted, "but I do not consider he would do so. If there exists a guilt, he has shared it in his deceiving, bilking, of Union officers. Look you, he will return. Twice, before, I have given him his *congé* due to a drunkenness, for which he has a weakness. Each time he returned and made a crawling on the knees to be restored to his wheel. He cannot do without Maison Galante. And Maison Galante—almost—cannot do without Edouard Janvier. In the matter of gaming, he is good, that one. *Oui*! he will return. If not this week, the next."

But Janvier did not return. After he'd been absent two weeks, Angelique sent a message to his home, summoning him to return and discuss their differences before she replaced him, only to learn that he had moved, and no one in his street had knowledge of his whereabouts. "*Ah, diable!*" Angelique exclaimed. "I know that Edouard. He has retired to one of his periodical intoxications." The matter was dismissed from her mind, after another croupier had been placed temporarily in his place as undermanager.

Tension and July heat increased throughout the city. At the end of the month a State Convention was held to consider giving the Negroes of Louisiana the vote. Clashes between whites and Negroes became more frequent. Rumors of a mysterious secret society of whites, known as the Southern Cross, with members sworn to oppose enfranchising the Negro, circulated through New Orleans. Haldane and Taggert, chafing at their confinement, no longer left Maison Galante to stroll the *banquettes*; they had no desire to become embroiled in some fracas involving whites and blacks.

Any fresh trouble arising now in New Orleans could result only in additional troops being moved in to occupy the city, with a concomitant establishment of still more rigid restrictions. Should some Federal authority suddenly conceive the idea of investigating movements of suspected British vessels . . . But Angelique refused to allow herself to dwell long on that possibility.

July was ending its third week when a message arrived from Rupert Downson: he had made port in New Orleans, once more, and was at present outfitting *Perdita* for the return voyage to Jamaica. He proposed to meet Haldane the evening of July 31st and take on a cargo of baled cotton.

Spirits about Maison Galante brightened visibly but were immediately dampened when a message arrived, via the grapevine, that a concerted raid was planned by Union soldiers on certain houses of New Orleans, suspected of harboring unsurrendered Confederate soldiers who were being accused of fomenting rebellion in the city. Though they'd had no hand in such action, still Haldane and Taggert had never surrendered either. It was imperative that they go at once into hiding, and their personal effects concealed, that no evidence of their presence at Maison Galante might be suspected.

Angelique received this news with the contemptuous word, *"Ah, ça!"* and informed Haldane: "It is nothing about which you are to discompose yourself, *comprende?* These raids are of a periodical happening ever since the surrender of New Orleans. Sometimes in one section of the city, sometimes in another. I will consider the proper arrangement."

The matter was disposed of easier than Haldane had hoped: he and Taggert went to stay with an aged French couple, Confederate sympathizers, who conducted a vegetable garden for a livelihood, some distance out Tchoupitoulas Road. Three days passed quickly while Haldane and Taggert tried to pay for their keep by working about the garden, cultivating and weeding. On the third night they were awakened from their pallet beds in the barn by one of Angelique's servants who brought word it was safe to return; the raids had proved of a minor nature; no soldier had even approached Maison Galante.

Haldane and Taggert decided to return at once. It was after three in the morning when they left the horses at the nearby livery stable, hurried along darkened streets, passed through a deserted courtyard, and, silently, let themselves in through the hidden doorway in the rear wall of Maison Galante. The whole house was dark when they arrived. Still weary from their broken sleep and the return ride, they crossed the courtyard and ascended the stairway to their rooms. Briefly, Haldane had contemplated rousing Angelique, then, deciding against it, undressed and went to bed.

He fell asleep almost at once. The hours passed. He dreamed that he heard Lustrous Candent down in the courtyard, pleading with Laure Gabriel to hurry, that time was slipping past.

". . . an y'all ain't got but ten-fifteen minutes moah to cotch dat paddle-steameh, Miss Laure, ma'am. Dat ol' *Glenmora Maid* boat ain' want no dee-lays when she gits ready cross dat Mississippi, ain' wait on nobuddy when he blows she whissle. An' y'all got recklek dem hawsses of Boaz's, dey don' sprout no wings—"

"Yes, Lustrous, I quite understand. Just as soon as Angelique brings me my . . ."

The words of the dream were lost; anyway, that couldn't have been Laure's drawling voice. Haldane tossed disappointedly on his bed.

Abruptly, his eyes popped open. Through his louvered door he saw full daylight had arrived. He jerked to a sitting position. The small clock across the room told him it was seven-thirty. "By God! That was no dream! It was real! I did hear voices down in the courtyard." And on second thought: "Not exactly Laure's, though." And yet, whoever it was had been called Laure, by Lustrous.

He leaped out of bed, dashed to the door, then

swung back to seize a dressing robe. He struggled into it, fingers fumbling with the frogs that held it closed. His hands made a hurried effort to smooth down his rumpled tawny hair as he jerked back the door and stepped swiftly to the balcony railing, eager gaze darting to the courtyard below.

Disappointment swept through him. No! No Laure Gabriel was to be seen below. Some other woman—a girl in a traveling costume of blue, designed with a high bodice. Very neat and trim, she looked. Over one arm was a light cloak, and tilted forward on her head, only partially covering the smoothly arranged blonde corn-silk hair, was a perky bonnet of braided straw, with a rolling brim and a tiny blue ostrich plume. She was standing just below the balcony, head turned in the direction of the big entrance doors.

No, it wasn't Laure Gabriel. Haldane's dream had confused him. He straightened from the balcony railing, still wiping sleep from his eyes. Then he halted. What had he been expecting, that she'd wear that faded calico forever? He looked again. Lustrous, dressed in his best, had come dashing back from the street, anxiety plain on his perspiring black features. He skidded to a stop, seized the telescope bag at the girl's feet.

"Com'awn, Miss Laure; we'uns got ter mek haste. Dat steameh don' wait—" He glanced up, catching sight of Haldane on the balcony. "Mawnin', Majuh, suh—mawnin' an' good-bye.

Time's a-gallupin'. We sees y'all in Taixus one of dese days—"

Haldane scarcely heard him. The girl's face lifted toward the balcony and he saw again the eyes of cornflower blue, as she raised a net-gloved hand in greeting, and heard her voice—but, surely, that wasn't Laure Gabriel's voice, those even, properly modulated tones: "Good morning, Major Haldane. It is very nice to see you again."

"Laure! Laure Gabriel!" he half yelled. It was unbelievable! Gone the faded calico, the grimy bare feet, the snarled hair. He found himself leaning far over the railing, staring. With an effort he controlled his emotions. "And it is a pleasure to see you again, Miss Gabriel—it is Miss Laure Gabriel, isn't it? I hope you've been well"—a smile twitched his lips—"and studying hard on your Byron. I must say it seems queer to meet you here, after—"

Laughter rose to her lips. "Indeed, yes, Major Haldane. I quite agree. Oh, yes, Lord Byron has been a great help." Her blue eyes dancing, she quoted:

*"A strange coincidence to use a phrase
'By which such things are settled nowadays.' "*

"Exactly what is settled?" he chuckled, and heard her reply:

"Farewell, a word that must be and has been—
A sound that makes us linger—yet—farewell—"

For a moment he was conscious only of Laure Gabriel's full rich tones. Then, "Not farewell, Laure—no! Must we always be saying farewell—?" He paused, suddenly aware of his appearance, the tousled hair, unshaven face, bare feet. Laure was already turning toward the street in answer to Lustrous' frantic pleas to hurry. Haldane protested, "Laure, wait! I'll get dressed—be right down—"

He swung back toward his room as Angelique emerged from her doorway. "Garth! You have returned. Until I heard your voice I did not know—" She was throwing a light shawl about her shoulders. "It is good you are able to see Laure, if only for a minute. *Helas*! She makes to depart almost the instant she has arrived—"

"I'll hurry," Haldane called over one shoulder. Angelique was descending to the courtyard, as he dove into his room, whipping off the robe. Water was splashed on his face. He struggled into his trousers and shirt. Next socks, shoes and a hasty brushing of tangled hair.

Even as he leaped down the stairway to the courtyard, he heard swift sounds of horses' hoofs and carriage wheels bumping over paving stones along Dauphine Street. He halted abruptly. No, it wouldn't be safe to be seen emerging from

Maison Galante in full daylight. Isham's spies might be loitering about. Anyway, he'd only make a spectacle of himself running through the streets after a carriage, even if there were a possibility of reaching the wharves before Laure's ship cast off.

A servant was closing the big doors. Angelique was returning through the passageway. "Garth, it is to be regretted Laure could no longer extend the visit. She made to arrive only last night. I did not dream you would return so late—"

"But—but, Angelique, what have you done to her?"

Angelique stared. "*Moi*? I have done nothing. What is it you suspect that I do?"

"No"—Haldane felt confused—"of course it has nothing to do with you. But no amount of studying Byron could effect such a change. I can't understand it. She was raw, uneducated, a hinterlander, the beautiful hair a mess most of the time, her bare feet rarely clean. In a patched and faded, threadbare calico. Now, suddenly, she is changed, a poised young woman, neat, no slurred speech. It—it is incredible!"

Angelique's eyes were round. "You do not know?"—as though she couldn't quite believe him ignorant of various happenings.

"Know what?" he demanded.

Abruptly, Angelique went into peals of laughter. "Oh, my Garth! This is of a most humorous. As you say, of an incredibility. She deceives you to a completeness during those weeks at the Boar and Tankard. Did I not maintain she was a smart one, our Laure? She accommodates any role to a perfection."

"Role?" Haldane's jaw dropped. "You—you mean, Laure's an actress?"

"Before the war, she effects a touring of the larger cities of the South with Burnstock's Shakesperian Players. You did not know? But, no, how could you? She was sworn to secrecy."

"I'll be blasted!"

"Always, she has had this enthusiasm for this English poet, Lord Byron. How many times I have endeavour' to create in her the interest for Baudelaire. His *Fleurs du Mal.* But, *non.* Always she retains this enthusiasm for the Lord Byron."

"But why did she have to leave so soon? Judd will be disappointed when he wakes, not to have seen her."

"Garth"—a trifle impatiently—"you still do not believe the war continues? Laure was compelled to leave. She is under orders. If certain news from Washington is of a verity, then, in this business of Reconstruction, the North will act with a complete malevolence in your State of Texas. Laure Gabriel will be of much use there. Who knows? I may also be sent to your Texas—" She broke off, smiled. "Come with me and I will give you breakfast. We shall speak more of this Reconstruction of a complete hideousness."

The following day, Robert delivered to Angelique a message some strange Negro had brought to the entrance of Maison Galante. The message was verbal and to the effect that Big Indigo had suffered an injury that would prevent his coming to Maison Galante for a few days at least. Angelique went to Haldane's room at once. "But what sort of injury?" Haldane frowned. "Will Big Indigo get here in time to guide Judd and me to the coffee house, for us to be there when Downson arrives in *Perdita*?"

"That I do not think," Angelique replied promptly. "Otherwise, why his concern to send us this message? Ah, *mon Dieu*, something is always making an annoyance. What? No, Robert did not know the man who delivered the message. Of a probability it arrived in a roundabout manner, doubtless relayed through some fisherman contacted by Big Indigo. My poor Indigo—it is to be hoped his injury is not of a seriousness."

Haldane persisted, where would Big Indigo find this theoretical fisherman? Angelique explained: "There is scattered through those small islands of Breton Sound, a kind of settlement of Negro-Choctaw Indian people who make the living with fishing and trapping. It would be most simple to seek out such a one to deliver a message."

Haldane's frown deepened. "Good Lord! And you thought your cotton-house was secret, with fishermen plying all through those waters? I'm just surprised it hasn't already been uncovered—"

"*Allons donc*! You speak a nonsense, my Garth. These fishermen need bring you no disconcern. Such types have no interest in politics or war. They are of the most primitive and exist only to fish and trap the muskrat. If by chance they saw the cotton-house, it would afford them no thought. They are not interested in cotton bales."

"Even so—" Haldane paused. "Great Scott! I'm to meet Downson the night of the 31st. I could never find my way through that swamp and neither could Judd."

"Do not discompose yourself. I know the route. Not so well as Big Indigo, perhaps, but almost. Of a certainty I can lead you and M'sieu Taggert there. Except that I will require more of time. Wait! It would be of the most indiscreet should we ride openly from New Orleans by daylight. *Non*! We shall be forced to leave by night. Before dawn of the 30th. That will allow time of the most ample, should I perhaps, stray from the route. Always, previously when visiting the cotton-house I have taken my barouche, as though to ride for an airing. When the carriage had traveled as far as possible, I made the change of clothing and continued, with Big Indigo, by horseback, while Boaz arranged his return for my ride back. This time I shall go all the journey by saddle. With you, my Garth,"—her white teeth flashed—"it should be of the most enjoyable. *Parbleau*! You do not listen."

Haldane apologized, explaining he was still wondering about Big Indigo's injury. Angelique agreed. "You are correct. With business of a most serious before us, I think only of pleasure. I am an insane one! As to the injury, it cannot be too serious. Otherwise, Indigo would have informed us of its nature. Is it, you do not trust to my guidance? Have no fear, I shall find the way. Of a certainty."

It was still three hours from dawn, the morning of the 30th, when Angelique, Haldane and Taggert emerged through the hidden door at the rear of the house, to find Robert waiting with horses, on Bourbon Street. Angelique had donned her long cloak and broad-brimmed felt hat, pulled low. She wore man's clothing and the high boots. They climbed silently into saddles and moved rapidly through the silent streets.

CHAPTER 15

Fortunately, Angelique had allowed extra time for the journey. She had not exaggerated in her confession she was less familiar than Big Indigo with the route to the cotton-house. Now, landmarks she'd counted on were overgrown with rank vegetation, certain trails were completely under water. Three times she lost her way, and Haldane and Taggert, naturally, were unable to help her. Their first night was spent in the swamp after devouring hungrily the food they had brought; the remaining hours of the night were spent in fighting mosquitoes.

A mosquito-netting wrapped about Angelique's head lessened to some extent the torment; nevertheless, the journey was difficult, and there was an increasing admiration in Haldane and Taggert for her refusal to evince the slightest weakening. Contrarily, she maintained an unflagging show of spirits, poking fun at what she insisted on terming her stupidity in straying from the route. The following morning, after considerable floundering around in the swamp, Angelique recognized a certain twisted-branched cypress which symbolized a marking to set them on the correct way. It was dusk when they arrived at the dark and deserted cotton-house.

The absence of Big Indigo and his two Negro assistants furnished an immediate basis for speculation, while they were tethering the horses to a low-hanging live-oak limb. Haldane led the way to the cotton-house and found the door on the inland side closed, but unlocked. After some fumbling about the gloomy interior they found a five-gallon can of coal oil from which they filled and then lighted the lamp. The place appeared much as Haldane had seen it last: there were a pair of bunks, with rumpled blankets, built against each side wall. The crude wooden table stood as before; straight-back chairs were scattered about. A few dirty dishes, some cigar butts and a nearly empty bottle of brandy stood on the deal table. At one side was a small cast-iron stove, its chimney disappearing through a hole, between rafters, in the slanting roof.

Taggert opened the stove door and thrust his hand among the ashes. "Ain't been no fire here for some time," he announced gloomily. He sauntered to the opposite end of the building, between the shadow-blackened tiers of cotton bales, and returned with word that the far door was bolted. "But where's Big Indigo?" he grumbled.

"Angelique and I have concluded," Haldane replied, "in view of the fact that Big Indigo's horse is missing, that, despite his injury, he may have started for New Orleans." In that case,

Taggert wanted to know, why hadn't they met him on the way? "Judd, you're forgetting we got off the route a couple of times. He could have passed us then." Taggert conceded that seemed plausible. "Still," he insisted, "that don't tell us what become of his two Negro helpers."

"I think it almost a certainty," Angelique offered, "there has been a contact with fishermen in these parts. The two Negroes, doubtless, have gone to the fishermen for an enjoyment." She smiled. "These fishermen have families, daughters. Or, of a possibility, the Negroes found it a necessity to accompany Big Indigo to New Orleans, assist to hold him in the saddle; the injury may be of a seriousness we do not suspect. It makes one to worry of his condition." Haldane inquired if it were likely the two Negroes would leave on foot? Angelique nodded. "*Naturellement*, if Big Indigo required the aid they could afford."

"I don't like it," Taggert stated moodily, but he couldn't explain why when asked for details. Unconsciously, the sergeant's right hand dropped to the cap-and-ball at his side, as he suggested it might be a good idea for Haldane to have his six-shooter handy to reach.

Haldane nodded shortly. "My gun'll be ready if I need it. Stop your fretting. Even if the Negroes aren't here, you and I can help Downson and his men load the cotton aboard, when he shows up."

"So much is settled," Angelique interposed. "For one, I am famished. Let us determine what food those lazy Negroes have left for us." Her brows lifted as she surveyed the table. "At least they have lived high, those black ones. Brandy! Cigars! I think I shall threaten to have them whipped. Except that they would not believe me." Going to the small pine cupboard, nailed to one wall, she produced potatoes, a chunk of bacon, coffee, some dried apples in a paper sack, and a tin of crackers. There were also, she announced, a second bottle of brandy, nearly full, and a cigar box with a few smokes remaining. A half-filled bucket of water stood in one corner. Glancing toward the single window, near the cupboard, Angelique asked if it were too dark to find firewood.

Brief vestiges of waning light remained when Taggert and Haldane stepped out. By the time they'd returned, after gathering a double armful of dead branches from beneath trees, it had grown completely dark, and a few stars were winking into being overhead. Angelique had put aside her cloak and hat; her shining chestnut hair wrapped in a blue madras bandanna, she was busying herself with cooking utensils. Haldane built up the fire in the small stove, and potatoes, sliced thin, were set to frying, Taggert mean-while restlessly pacing the length of the building between the stacked cotton bales. Finally he returned to the stove and after standing helplessly about for a minute, announced that while food was being prepared, he'd take a walk down to the shore to see if there was any sign of *Perdita*'s arrival. Haldane said, "I figure it's a bit early to expect Downson, but perhaps not. Judd, you'd best take a lantern. Wait, I'll light it."

"I don't reckon to need no lantern," Taggert answered. "The sound of the waves will lead me right. Coming back, there'll be enough light through the window to show the way."

"Do not remain too long away, M'sieu Taggert." Angelique glanced up from the stove, tiny beads of moisture dotting her forehead. "Sooner than you may suspect, food will be prepared." Taggert nodded dourly and departed, closing the door behind him. Angelique observed, "He is nervous as a cat, that one. There is nothing to fear, but he is—how do you say?—on his edge."

Frowning, Haldane replied, "Something's biting at him. As to being edgy, I've known Judd since we were kids. Sometimes, I think he has second-sight. Generally, when he gets this way, there is trouble in the offing, though it may be days away. If I didn't believe you know conditions, hereabouts, I might be on edge myself."

Angelique's dimples appeared. "So! You trust to me your life. It gives me to be proud, Garth. Such confidence merits a brandy." She procured the bottle from the cupboard and poured liquor into two glasses. "Now, an *aperitif*, no? With the food, we have another, in place of wine." They sipped their brandies slowly. An aroma of coffee permeated the air. Haldane dropped into a chair, watching Angelique's movements about stove and table. He remarked amusedly that she'd make a very handsome man—though thank God she wasn't; what was most astounding, he continued, was that with her other varied accomplishments, she could also cook.

"*Pouf!*" Angelique exclaimed. "In the *cuisine* all French women excel. One day I shall prepare for you a *bouillabaisse* or a *daube glacé* that will perform of a melting in your mouth. Then, M'sieu Garth Haldane, you will concede the admittance I have remaining at least one virtue."

She flashed a quick, mischievous glance. The heat from the stove, the weariness induced by the journey through the swamps, combined to bring a lassitude to Haldane, as he lazily informed her she was the most virtuous woman he knew.

"In such event, it is most clear you have not known many women. But for what you say, my Garth, I am of the most appreciating. Truly you are again, tonight, of the deep South. Of a verity!"

Food was placed on the table, coffee and fresh brandy poured. Haldane mentioned Judd's absence; he should be coming in any minute.

Angelique said, "The fragrance of coffee

211

may bring him soon." She rounded the table, resting one slim white hand fondly on Haldane's shoulder a moment, before seating herself across from him. They'd been eating for five minutes when Haldane again mentioned Taggert. "I'll step outside and give him a hail." He was about to rise when a step sounded at the door, and Haldane sank back in his chair. "There's Judd, now." A certain relief showed in his tones.

CHAPTER 16

The door opened quickly and as quickly closed again, after admitting an individual, a complete stranger to Haldane, who moved with astonishing agility, considering his toad-like bulk. He wore the blue uniform of a Union colonel, and there was a leveled Colt's revolver in his fist.

"Just stay as you are, please, Major Haldane, and keep your hands above the table—"

"Colonel Isham!" Angelique gasped, her face ashen.

"Exactly, my dear Madame Galante. And what a charming domestic scene I've witnessed through the window. The monsieur home from the day's toil, the madame, with the humble meal prepared—No, no, Major Haldane! I won't take kindly to such stealthy moves. Please remain as you are, with your hands—empty—on the table. Madame Galante, don't you think you should formally present me? Naturally, I'm perfectly aware of Major Haldane's identity, even without his gray uniform. Still, the social amenities should be observed. Where are the polished French manners of New Orleans society of which I've heard so much—?"

Haldane interrupted curtly to remark that any introduction was superfluous; in fact, having already heard too much of Colonel Albro Isham, he was positive he didn't care to be introduced. No gentleman, Haldane pointed out in a cold insolent tone, could possibly be interested in meeting one of an inferior breed. All the time he was talking, Haldane's mind was occupied with the six-shooter at his belt, below the top of the table, speculating as to the best method of throwing Isham off guard long enough to . . .

"It won't do, Major," Isham remarked in an amused tone. "I refuse to get angry at such taunts and lose my head. You Southerners are all alike. You thought to win a war with your culture, your swords-and-romance-and-flowers attitude. You weren't, in short, realistic. There is nothing at all practicable about you."

He stood just within the doorway, a few yards from the table, his spindling legs in boots spread wide apart below the enormous belly bulging below the belt-line. Fleshy jowls sagged below his uniform coat collar. His head, so much as could be seen below the brim of the black slouch hat, was apparently devoid of hair. He had no mustache; his eyebrows, lashes, were practically colorless. His shoulders appeared to commence just below the small ears; the cheeks were incredibly pink and smooth. An extremely dangerous individual, Haldane concluded, and one not to be underestimated, despite his absurd appearance. The man possessed cunning, ruthlessness.

Colonel Isham continued, voice suave, almost mannerly, "I can perceive, Major Haldane, that you have mentally been comparing your physical aspects with mine, to—oh, I cheerfully concede this—to my disadvantage. Therein, without doubt, lies the secret of your success with the charming Madame Galante. The sole advantage I possess is this extremely efficient bit of mechanism manufactured by Mr. Samuel Colt, which I feel sure quite balances—"

"*Que diable!*" Angelique's voice shook with cold fury. "Enough of senseless talk, Colonel Isham. What have you done with Big Indigo and my other Negroes? How did you perform a locating of my cotton-house? What are your intentions? One demands an answer. Instantly!"

"You demand?" Colonel Isham chuckled, the sound gurgling deeply in the depths of his gross neck. "Really, Madame Galante, this, you force me to state, is not your evening for demanding anything. However, I can appreciate your curiosity. And Major Haldane's." He made a sort of squat bow in Haldane's direction, but never for an instant was there the slightest relaxing of his alertness; the revolver continued to point as steadily at Haldane's body.

His chuckle was repeated. "I have the honor of relieving your curiosity, madame—sir!" Again the caricature of a bow, his pink lips smiling wetly. "Ah, yes, your Big Indigo. I had sent to you a message regarding his regrettable injury. Somewhat prematurely, I confess. Actually, the injury didn't occur until later. As to your other help, they proved stubborn and would give no information. We were forced to hang them, a short way from here. It was only after the hanging that Big Indigo consented to show us the best route through the swamps. Fortunately I had his horse, or he might have got clean away, after he had misled us. My first shot broke his leg—the injury I mentioned a moment ago. I was forced also to kill him, like a horse with a broken leg, you understand. It is all most regrettable. . . . Later, when we spied you heading this way, we decided to withdraw from view until you'd entered the cotton-house."

A drumming anger had commenced in Garth Haldane's head. He speculated as to whether a quick draw of his gun would be successful. And where the devil was Judd?

Isham's voice intruded. "Major Haldane, you are doubtless puzzled as to the whereabouts of your comrade. Of course, you have been expecting him to take me from behind in a very dramatic rescue. I advise that you give up any such hope. It's no use. Another regrettable accident, I'm sorry to say. Taggert—I believe that's his name—had progressed but a short distance from this building, when he was struck on the head by some heavy object. It seemed to incapacitate him. At present he is asleep, down near the shore, with my men to guard his slumbers.

"They happen also to be waiting for a certain Rupert Downson, a Britisher, to put in an appearance. Once we've captured Mr. Downson, and the cotton bales have been removed, Washington will have certain representations to make at London. It will be most enjoyable to watch the limeys squirm. The English caused us considerable annoyance all through the war . . ."

Haldane was scarcely listening now. Judd was out of the fight. Nothing could be expected from him. Some other plan must be worked out.

"Janvier!" Angelique exclaimed suddenly. "It was he who furnished the information about us, this cotton, everything!"

"You've guessed at last!" Isham laughed delightedly. "Why, of course, it was Janvier. He proved quite useful to me—oh, so very much so. It appears you hurt his feelings, dear Madame Galante. I assured him I could understand that. He talked most freely. You were cruel to him. You not only repulsed his honorable advances, but sacked him from his position as well."

Colonel Isham shook an admonishing finger at Angelique. "An extremely indiscreet manner in which to treat a sensitive soul like Edouard Janvier. You should have remembered he was fully aware of your activities. And Major Haldane's. Or should I say, especially Major Haldane's?"

He wagged his head and uttered reproving, clucking sounds. "For a time, Madame Galante, you had me completely fooled. I had even begun to doubt you possessed hidden cotton. It was ever a weakness of mine to be like jelly in the hands of a charming woman—"

Angelique's laugh rose on a caustic note. "There is nothing further you have left to say, when you admit you are like the jelly."

"Doubtless, you are correct," Isham replied imperturbably, "but we were speaking of Janvier, weren't we? He assured me you owned this cotton, but—stupid dolt!—could only furnish the vaguest idea as to the hidden location. And so, at his suggestion, I spread word to the fishermen throughout these islands, that a reward of one hundred dollars would be paid to the first man to locate this place—you understand, a hundred dollars is a fortune to such ignorant people. It wasn't long before one fellow brought me and three troopers here in a skiff. But such a roundabout way. It was dreadful. Swamp, mosquitoes. And all that nasty slimy water. And then your help were so belligerent about showing us a more direct route. So we've waited each day in the hope you'd arrive, drawn by news I sent by a fisherman, regarding Big Indigo's injury—a truly lamentable affair—his accident—"

"That Janvier!" Angelique's foot stamped the floor beneath the table. "I promise you, I shall make this Janvier suffer for this treachery he has accomplished!"

"Allow me to contradict you," Isham stated. "You'll do nothing of the sort. Poor Janvier! He insisted on sharing equally any money I intend to receive for this contraband cotton. I assure you, I did my best to dissuade him, but he was obstinate. It became necessary to arrest him as an enemy of the United States. I, myself, commanded the detachment escorting him to prison, in the hope I might, finally, convince him of his error. Either he tried to escape, or his foot slipped when he was stepping from the *banquette*, at a crossing. There was that sudden movement, you understand. I couldn't chance losing a prisoner. I shot him. Instantly."

Stark horror was mirrored in Angelique's dark eyes. Haldane had but half listened to the words passing between them, as various plans revolved through his head, only to be as swiftly discarded. Isham had stated he had arrived with three men in a skiff. Three infantrymen probably. Not counting Angelique, that made one against four. A clean shot at Isham would lessen the odds. The three soldiers were down by the shore.

Angelique had recovered her voice, her tones carrying the utmost contempt. "No, Colonel Isham, you did not kill Edouard Janvier for fear of an escape. You killed him because he knew too much concerning your thieveries, and to retain for yourself, alone, the money you plan to gain through his disclosures."

She reached for the brandy bottle on the table, the neck of the bottle clattering against the edge of the glass as she poured one of the tumblers nearly full. Liquor slopped over the rim of the glass as she carried it to her lips, barely moistening them before she again placed it on the table.

". . . and you state your facts very bluntly, dear Madame Galante," Isham was saying in injured tones.

"But at least they are facts, honest facts," Angelique snapped.

"Alas, lamentably so," Isham conceded. He was watching Haldane more closely now, his gun bearing directly on the major. "But, my dear madame, you must realize now that I am prepared to let nothing stand in the way of securing what I want. Including you, dear lady. And, of course"—nodding toward Haldane—"your major. Perhaps now we understand each other." Though he spoke to Angelique, never for an instant did his eyes leave Haldane.

"For longer than you would believe, I have understood you," Angelique spoke with a cold fury. *"Nom d'un chien*! You were of the most simple to understand. But, enough of this useless fencing. We concede you hold, for the moment, an upper hand. That much is settled. So! Now—you will allow Major Haldane, Sergeant Taggert and myself to depart. In return, I present you as a gift all the cotton you find here. That is of a most fairness, *n'est-ce pas*?"

Again the fat, slimy chuckle. "You forget one thing, dear Madame Galante. You cannot give me, as a gift or otherwise, that which you no longer own. I have already confiscated this cotton in the name of the United States Government—to be exact, the U.S. Treasury."

"I doubt," Haldane commented, level-voiced, "that your government will ever learn of it."

"Oh, quite possibly you are correct, Major Haldane," Isham said cheerfully, "but if I don't profit from the cotton in question, it will only fall into the hands of men in Washington who have never had the courage to don a uniform—the profiteers and other vultures gaining wealth through the war. Now, surely, you prefer that a brother officer, even an enemy—careful! Please do not move your hand in such fashion, Major Haldane, or I shall be forced to shoot. Just keep both hands in sight on the table. Or was that twitching of your fingers involuntary, prompted, perhaps, by a desire to close them about my throat? I shouldn't, were I you, attempt anything rash. My trigger requires only the slightest pressure. My gun has been known to explode a charge on very little provocation. So, please just sit quietly and turn over in your mind various devices by which you may turn the tables on me. I do not object. Not at all. And speaking of tables, just in case you've contemplated over-turning the table, lamp and all, and plunging us into sudden darkness, I shouldn't advise it. I am quite certain that any sudden movement on your part would startle me into shooting. And there we have it," he concluded smoothly. "Madame Galante, have you any further suggestions to offer?"

Again, Angelique carried the brandy to her dry lips, every nerve straining to keep her voice under control. "Perhaps it will save time to listen to any suggestion you are prepared to offer, Colonel Isham."

"Now I consider that most sensible," Isham purred triumphantly. "It is, to be brief, a complete acknowledgment of defeat. You have admitted I hold all the high cards. This is most delightful. I had anticipated difficulties." Angelique inter-posed a sharp suggestion that he get down to business. "Ah, yes, thank you. Business, of course. So! In the first place, Major Haldane occupies a very untenable position. I understand, from Janvier, that he has never negotiated a formal surrender to our forces, nor taken the Oath of Allegiance to the United States. This I consider deplorable. The penalty is, of course, death upon capture. The same condition applies to Sergeant Taggert."

Angelique's fingers about the glass of brandy tightened until the nails showed white. Isham continued, "But I'm inclined to be lenient. At bottom, I'm a very tender-hearted man. I believe it could be arranged for the major and his sergeant to be transported to Texas, were certain conditions observed. I would not even insist on the Oath. I'm a broad-minded man. Defeat rankles and I would not expect our enemies to embrace us—"

"I do not think," Haldane interrupted harshly, "that I could carry out *any* conditions *you* might offer—"

"A moment, Garth," Angelique cut in. "We shall hear what he has to say. This yet may not prove to be an undoing of a completeness. Please to continue, Colonel Isham. The conditions you offer?"

"My connection with your gambling parlor," Isham went on, "has been most profitable. However, under the circumstances, it could be made more so—"

"You demand of a larger share of winnings, is it not?" Angelique said tersely. "I do not argue. What is it you wish?"

"Shall we say a seventy-five and a twenty-five percent division? To me, the seventy-five, of course." Angelique flashed him a look of hate, but agreed in a cold voice to the proposition. There was nothing else to do, she admitted. At the same time, she insisted, the new arrangement not become effective until Major Haldane and Taggert were safe on Texas soil; she made it clear she did not trust Colonel Isham.

"Oh, that is very satisfactory," Isham said ingratiatingly. "You are very generous, dear Madame Galante. I now have your cotton and seventy-five percent of Maison Galante's profits. It seems impossible I should ask more, doesn't it? I fear you'll think me greedy."

Angelique had again been on the point of raising the brandy glass to her ordeal-parched lips. Now she paused, puzzled. "There remains still more you demand?" she asked unbelievingly.

Isham didn't reply at once, though his gun barrel tilted a trifle on Haldane. "It is," he commenced apologetically, "a rather delicate matter to propose in Major Haldane's presence. I could wish he were absent." He sighed regretfully. "If I offend, Major, I'm sure you'll appreciate my position."

Though his gaze remained on Haldane, he addressed himself to Angelique. "You have, dear Madame Galante, in the past been extremely unkind to me in various ways. Under the circumstances, it appears no more than just that you grant me privileges at least equal to those enjoyed by Major Haldane. I'm sure I could be most comfortable at Maison Galante—Don't try it, Major!" Isham's voice suddenly went harsh, as he noticed the stiffening of Haldane's form.

And in that instant, Angelique with a deft movement of her right hand, sent her tumbler of brandy flying straight toward Colonel Albro Isham's face.

CHAPTER 17

Occupied as he was with Haldane, Isham almost missed Angelique's maneuver, though even before the glass struck, splashing stinging liquor into the small pig eyes, there came an involuntary swerving of the gun barrel, followed by the abrupt flash of orange fire. The detonation was instantly accompanied by a second thundering report from Haldane's cap-and-ball Colt. Isham coughed chokingly and swayed like a stricken boar. Haldane fired a second time, as he came up out of his chair.

A succeeding bullet from Isham's gun flew wild and ploughed through the tin of coal oil standing near the tiered bales of cotton. A soft gurgling of escaping oil formed an undertone for the clatter of Isham's weapon as it dropped from his nerveless fist. Haldane pushed away from the table and, deliberately, triggered a third shot into Colonel Isham's quivering body.

Clawing frantically at his blinded eyes, Isham took three stumbling, half-running, steps toward Haldane, faltered, and went plunging at a tangent across the table, which gave way under his bulk, the lighted lamp hurtling through the air to land, with a crash of splintered glass, in the rapidly forming pool of coal oil seeping across the plank floor. Isham was screaming now, as he lay sprawled on the debris of the table, the tones carrying a queer, inhuman, squealing tone. Then, quite suddenly, he became quiet.

There ensued a moment of almost complete darkness, before the flickering wick of the oil lamp ignited the coal oil. Then came a swift rush of flame throwing into bold relief the occupants of the cotton-house.

Angelique sat as before, all color drained from her features, her head bent toward the huge inert bulk stretched lifeless, face down, at her feet, among the wreckage of splintered table and broken crockery. Haldane replaced his gun in holster, stepped quickly across the floor and, scooping up the revolver Isham had dropped, thrust it into his belt. An odor of burned black powder, smoke, combined with blazing coal oil, permeated the atmosphere. The flames along the floor had commenced to lick at the nearest bales of cotton.

Haldane grasped Angelique's arm. "Hurry! We've got to get out of here. The whole place is going up in flames. By this time Isham's soldiers have heard the shooting and—" He paused at the look in the shocked, white face turned up to him.

"It is that I am unable to stand, Garth. There is something bad that has happened to my legs. I have nothing of feeling in them."

Only then did Haldane realize she had been

struck by Isham's first bullet. He saw now the wet hole in the black sateen shirt, low and just above the hip. It required a moment for Haldane to realize exactly what this meant, before he started to lift her in his arms. An abrupt, agonized gasp was torn from her lips, and he quickly lowered her to the chair again. "I am so regretful, Garth. It does not pain me too greatly, only it is I can not stand the pain to be moved . . ." Her eyes closed.

Haldane glanced helplessly about. Isham's bullet must have reached her spinal cord, making her legs useless. Beyond them, the flames covered all one side of a bale of cotton and were crawling higher. It would be impossible to remain much longer. Outside, near the doorway, a voice called loudly for Colonel Isham. Haldane glanced quickly at the closed door, then retrieved the brandy bottle from the floor. Most of the liquor spilled out, but a little remained. He held the mouth of the bottle to Angelique's lips. "We're going to have to make a run for it. Try to stand the pain until we get outside, among the trees. Once there, we'll have a chance."

He gathered her carefully into his arms, endeavouring not to hear the poignant cry she made, and started across the floor. He fumbled awkwardly at the door knob, holding her as gently as possible while he worked at the catch. He caught the edge of the door with his booted toe and swung it back. Yells from the darkness beyond greeted their appearance. A repeating rifle bullet smashed into the door-jamb. Haldane moved back as a second shot ploughed through the window pane. With one foot he kicked shut the door, retreating back into the building. The flames leaped higher now, fanned by the brief rush of air from the doorway; at one side the fire neared the roof. Once the highly inflammable cotton was thoroughly ignited, the conflagration would travel swiftly through the entire structure.

Glancing at Angelique in his arms, he saw she had mercifully fainted. Behind Haldane stretched the long corridor between the stacked tiers of baled cotton. The door at the farther end might furnish an escaping point. Turning, holding Angelique close, Haldane hurried along the passageway, toward the opposite end of the cotton-house, flames licking at them from a blazing bale as they passed.

A smothered groan burst from Haldane's lips as he reached the far end of the building. Someone was already battering at the door. He might have known, he told himself dully, that Isham's men would guess his intentions. There was more room back here; it was from this end of the building that the already shipped bales had been removed. Haldane laid Angelique gently down across a pair of lower bales. Her eyes were still closed, her features paper white. Then drawing his gun,

Haldane sent a shot crashing through the closed door.

Instantly, the battering at the door stopped, though Haldane had no way of knowing if his bullet had found a mark. The yelling without also ceased, and for a few moments there was nothing to be heard but the crackling roar of flames at the inland end of the doomed cotton-house. By now the bales on both sides, at that end, were blazing furiously, brightly lighting like a raging inferno—and closing off—the passageway along which Haldane had carried Angelique but a few minutes before.

He left the door through which he'd fired and returned to Angelique. If she were only able to run. His hand moved gently about the spot where Isham's bullet had entered and, remembering Isham's position at the moment of shooting, Haldane guessed the leaden slug had smashed her spine, without doubt. He felt for her heart but could detect no movement. In the light from the flames he could see her eyes were still closed, the long dark lashes motionless against the white cheeks. After a second or so, the hand on Angelique's heart felt a faint, tired throb, and her voice just reached him. "Garth, is our position . . . one of a hopelessness?"

He assured her on the contrary, everything was going to be all right. Within a few minutes they'd be leaving and her pain would have vanished. He wasn't too sure she'd heard him. He bent close to hear, above the increasing roaring of flames, the next words she spoke: "Mine was a good trick . . . that of the brandy glass . . . no? I knew you would be swift . . . to take an advantage."

Heat and smoke swirling along the passage-way were suffocating. Haldane stepped to the door and drew back the bolt, without opening it, then returned to Angelique and slipped one arm gently under her shoulders. She spoke again, drowsily, "Garth, you have said to me . . . so many wonderful things. You have told me I was beautiful. You have sworn . . . you idolized me. You have spoken . . . of your great adoration . . . but never once have you told me you loved me . . ."

Haldane's voice was very unsteady as he told her he loved her more than anything in the world, that he'd love her always. A ghost of a smile touched her lips, her dark eyes fondly searching his features. "Ah, my Garth," she sighed, "that was a most beautiful lie . . . but I will believe you, because it makes me so warm within . . . and I become of the most cold." She essayed a small laugh. "That is queer, no . . . with so much of flame around? But this cold that possesses me . . . you will drive away, I know. You will hold me close . . . and keep telling me those so beautiful lies, while I think of all . . . our happy times. So many . . ."

Garth Haldane realized quite suddenly she was gone.

He lowered her gently back to the bale and stood erect. He had not noticed how the fire had advanced. There was a roaring from above as though the whole roof was ablaze. Smoke swirled into his lungs, and he leaned against the nearest bale, coughing, reluctant even now to leave the silent slim form so motionless on the cotton-bales.

The heat was intense. A jagged fork of flame licked down from the ceiling. Sparks showered about him. He slapped at spots on his shirt where blazing bits of wood started tiny flames. The smoke, the heat, were making him faint. Flames were licking now about the bales where Angelique lay. "A pyre for a gallant lady," he muttered thickly, and stood there, swaying groggily, not wanting to leave, his mind remembering . . .

There came a crashing and flames about his body. A section of blazing timber struck one shoulder, knocking him to the floor. He struggled feebly a moment to arise, then dropped back, as a velvet curtain of black oblivion enveloped him.

CHAPTER 18

Garth Haldane's eyes opened slowly. At either side were shadows, but directly overhead he saw small drifting clouds in a moonlit sky. He heard unaccustomed sounds, not at once definable, sounds reminiscent of those made by creaking masts and rigging of a moving ship. Then, feeling the slow rise and fall of a deck beneath his body, he realized he was actually at sea. Footsteps passed a few yards off; he caught muted voices, but before he could speak, they had passed on. There was a blanket covering him; he pushed it away.

One hand went to his head. The skin, in places, was painfully tender, as were spots on his hands. Something greasy had been spread over such spots. His eyebrows, mustache, hair, had a crisp, singed condition. The odor of smoke lingering in his nostrils, mingled with occasional wafts of tar and bilge water. His clothing was damp and held a scorched smell. Gradually his mind began to clear. After a minute he found there were blankets between him and the deck, a pillow beneath his head. His thoughts returned to the cotton-house. Angelique . . .

A shadowy figure took form, crouching at his side. "Garth?"

He recognized Judd Taggert's voice. "Yes," he said quietly. "Yes, Judd. Where are we?"

"Aboard the *Perdita*. Downson sure saved our skins for us—Garth, you feeling all right now?"

Haldane said in a stronger voice, "I'm all right, except that—" He didn't finish what he'd started: it was useless to ask questions regarding Angelique. "Exactly what happened, Judd? You mentioned Downson's saving our lives."

"And that's Gawd's truth. Do you recollect I left you and Angelique in the cotton-house, while I left for a walk to the shore? I'd only gone a short piece when some Yank bastuds jumped me from behind. Knocked me cold. Dragged me down to the shore to wait for Downson. That's how I figure it, leastwise—"

"You're probably right. It was Colonel Isham's men. He entered the cotton-house, caught us off guard, threw his six-shooter on me. Angelique made an opportunity for me, threw a glass of brandy in his face, outwitting him, giving me my chance. I killed him, but his shot went wild and . . . he hit her—" Haldane suppressed the groan that rose to his lips. After a moment he said more calmly, "The lamp got knocked over, into some spilled coal oil, started the place blazing. And there you were, knocked unconscious, down at the shore—"

"Trussed tighter'n a steer ripe for the brand-iron. About that time the *Perdita* arrived. Down-

234

son not getting any answering lantern signal, quick doused his lights. Then he heard shots and saw fire at the cotton-house. Him and his men grabbed guns, got into the rowboat and come ashore to investigate. One of the men stumbled over me when they got to the beach. By that time the Yank blue-bellies had left me and were at the cotton-house, which same was blazing like hell. Downson untied me, spilled water on me and brought me back to my senses, but I couldn't explain much that had happened. Couldn't tell Downson nothin' about you and Angelique."

He paused. Beneath them the deck slowly rose and fell. The tang of salt water filled Haldane's nostrils. He breathed deeply, feeling stronger. Sails flapped momentarily, then refilled. Taggert went on, "We closed in, sort of feeling our way, until we learned there was only three Yanks in blue uniforms near the house. The flames had broke through and the roof was ablaze. By that time it looked like the whole inland end of the cotton-house was gone. We figured they had you trapped at the other end."

"What about the Yanks?"

"Do I have to tell you we killed the bastuds?" Taggert asked harshly. "They opened fire on us, but we wa'n't in no mood to be stopped. One of Downson's hands released our hawsses, tied under the trees and let 'em fend for themselves. It looked like the trees near the building would catch fire, too, which same they did. Downson and me entered the sea end of the buildin', to learn if we could locate you and Angelique. That heat was awful. Lucky that rear door was unlocked. We found you, face down, when we got in, your clothes afire in spots. Angelique—" He stopped.

"You don't have to tell me, Judd. I know."

Taggert said gruffly, "She was all woman—and a lot more, Garth. Hell! I reckon I know how you feel." He continued after a moment. "We got you out just before the roof fell in, beat out the fire on your clothing and on your hair. Some of the spots kept smolderin', so when we got you to the shore, we doused you with water, then rowed back to the ship. It's going to take a spell before all your hair grows out like it was—"

"Where's Rupert Downson? I must thank him—"

"At the wheel, doin' the steerin'. He's sort of been stallin' around in circles, until we decide what we want to do. He's got men up in the bow for lookouts. Should any Yank gunboat have caught a glimpse of that fire, they might start investigatin' over this way. Downson wants to be ready to make a run for it."

"Where are we now?"

"Leavin' Breton Sound, he says, gettin' out toward the Gulf. The wind's freshenin'. Garth, we should be gettin' along to Texas. Downson tells me the Yanks plan to make an example of Texas, bear down real hard on us Texans and teach us a lesson we won't forget. I claim we can still whup 'em. There'll be work for us there, Garth. Laure Gabriel is already there. And there's White Hawk—"

Haldane interrupted, "Just what is Downson planning to do?"

"That's what I come to ask you. He's been sort of holdin' back. He says if you want to return to N'Awleans—"

Haldane propped himself up on elbows. "In God's name why should I want to go back to New Orleans?" His voice was tinged with anguish. "There's nothing there for me—now."

"Downson don't know how you feel, Garth. But he'd like for you to make up your mind. He says to tell you he can steer north by west—I think that was the way he put it—and run up the Mississippi to N'Awleans, or he can set his course due west, make port at Galveston, and drop us off there. That means Texas. What do I tell him, Garth, north by west, or due west?"

Haldane came to a sitting position. The wave of dizziness that swept over him quickly vanished. He sat motionless, eyes unseeing. Black shadows of masts and rigging slid easily across the deck with every wave that rolled the ship. Taggert was still waiting for an answer. Haldane struggled to his feet, the breeze fresh on his face as he came erect. Anxiously, Taggert stood close to his shoulder. Haldane made his way on unsteady legs to the railing and stood gazing astern, where a faint crimson glow still lingered in the night sky beyond Breton Sound. Gusts of salt spray struck his face. The starboard light made dancing reflections mixed with tiny gleams of phosphorescence in the oily hills of black water, sweeping smoothly past.

Haldane gripped the damp railing with both hands, the fingers of the right momentarily coming into contact with the jade ring on his left hand, bringing to memory her words, ". . . remember me, then . . ."

Taggert, at his shoulder, said anxiously, "Are you all right, Garth? Did you hear what I said? Downson wants to know—"

Haldane's eyes closed a moment, as though to ward off pain. When he opened them again, the sky glow beyond Breton Sound was fading. His voice was quiet, level-toned, when he answered Taggert. "Ask Mr. Downson to steer due west, please."

Center Point Large Print
600 Brooks Road / PO Box 1
Thorndike, ME 04986-0001 USA

(207) 568-3717

US & Canada:
1 800 929-9108
www.centerpointlargeprint.com